Midnight at the Shelter

Midnight at the Shelter

NANCI TURNER STEVESON

Quill Tree Books
An Imprint of HarperCollins Publishers

Quill Tree Books is an imprint of HarperCollins Publishers.

Midnight at the Shelter
Copyright © 2022 by Nanci Turner Steveson
All rights reserved. Printed in the United States of America.
No part of this book may be used or reproduced in any manner whatsoever
without written permission except in the case of brief quotations
embodied in critical articles and reviews. For information address
HarperCollins Children's Books, a division of HarperCollins Publishers,
195 Broadway, New York, NY 10007.
www.harpercollinschildrens.com

Library of Congress Cataloging-in-Publication Data
Names: Steveson, Nanci Turner, author.
Title: Midnight at the shelter / Nanci Turner Steveson.
Description: First edition. | New York : Quill Tree Books, [2022] |
    Audience: Ages 8-12. | Audience: Grades 4-6. | Summary: MahDi,
    a three-legged rescue dog, must risk everything to save his pack of
    shelter animals from an uncertain future.
Identifiers: LCCN 2022014455 | ISBN 9780062673213 (hardcover)
Subjects: CYAC: Dogs—Fiction. | Animals—Fiction. | Animal shelters—
    Fiction. | Animals with disabilities—Fiction. | LCGFT: Animal
    fiction.
Classification: LCC PZ7.1.S7454 Mi 2022 | DDC [Fic]—dc23
LC record available at https://lccn.loc.gov/2022014455

Typography by Kathy H. Lam
22 23 24 25 26 PC/LSCH 10 9 8 7 6 5 4 3 2 1
❖
First Edition

*For all the shelter animals waiting for
Just the Right Home. And to Luna, Quinn, Story,
Sufi, and Tink—who rescued us just when we
needed you the most.—N.T.S.*

*To John and Gill Dalley—My personal heroes and
cofounders of Soi Dog Foundation. —H.T.C.*

Midnight
at the
Shelter

CHAPTER 1

Mondays are full of surprises. MomDoc and I always work Mondays because it's the busiest day at a vet clinic. Crazy things happen over a weekend and the waiting room gets full with strange and sometimes funny problems. Like Fred the boxer, who spent Saturday night at an emergency clinic the next town over. His new dad wanted MomDoc to check him out and be sure the emergency place had given Fred the right treatment. Because everybody knows, MomDoc is the best vet.

Good thing my best terrier friend, Ozzie, was in the office and didn't get a close-up view of Fred's face. Ozzie didn't always have the best reaction to things that were frightening, and Fred definitely qualified as a fright.

I went to sit beside him in the waiting room.

Fred, buddy, what happened to you?

His face looked like a giant pimple, red and swollen. I couldn't even see his eyes. He lowered his head and tucked his tail.

Porcupine. Again.

Little pockmarks studded his muzzle where the quills had pierced his flesh. He was already missing half of one ear, but the porcupine had found its target and the part that was still there twitched. Fred's dad, whom MomDoc and I had picked out special for him, wrapped his hands around Fred's chest and half carried, half scooted him across the floor to check in at the counter. I followed.

Same porcupine? How'd it find you?

Dunno. Just did.

You went back into those woods again, didn't you.

Fred wouldn't look at me.

As I suspected. Lucky for you MomDoc can fix you up.

I hope so. I can't see nuthin' and it hurts. . . .

By the time Fred was called to the treatment room, the front of the clinic was filling up. Mrs. Peterson sat on one of the couches with her giant orange tabby cat, Marcus. He hissed at me.

Here's a rule: never get too close to a cat in a crate. They have claws that reach a lot farther than you'd ever guess. I know this from experience.

Marcus let out the kind of screech you'd expect to hear in the dark woods on the night of a full moon. A lady with a tiny Pomeranian wrapped in a fuzzy pink coat clutched the dog tight to her chest.

"What's wrong with that cat?"

She said it with a bit of an attitude, like her Pom had never sneezed once in her life.

"He has an infection," Mrs. Peterson said.

Marcus stood up, arched his back, and stared down at his feet. A pool of yellow fluid trickled out onto Mrs. Peterson's lap. She flew off the chair and held the crate far away from her body.

"Oh no!"

I ran to the treatment room in the back where MomDoc had Fred laid out on the exam table.

Ra-Ruuu! Emergency pee-pad needed—fast!

Ozzie tossed a stuffed penguin over the gate. It landed by my feet.

Pee-pad, not penguin!

Ooof. Sorry.

MomDoc came over and peeked through the door to the reception part of the clinic, then reached down and rubbed the top of my head.

"Good boy, MahDi. You keep things in order out there,

okay? I'll send help for Mrs. Peterson."

I bounced back over to the crate, which was now on the floor, to help calm Marcus down.

It's not your fault.

Marcus, being a cat, hissed at me. Cats are quite mysterious. After he and Mrs. Peterson went back for MomDoc to work her magic, our neighbor, Mrs. Peabody, came in.

"Come, come now my little cutie-patootie-scrumptious-little-sweetheart, come inside with Mummy."

Mrs. Peabody's hound, also named Peabody, was another one of MomDoc's and my matches from the shelter several years ago. Peabody was anything but little. He was rotund with squishy flesh and was often tormented by young kids who liked to poke him and giggle when their fingers left an indent. The only *patootie*-related thing about him was what came out of his rear end on a fairly consistent basis.

Peabody did not want to come in and had parked himself just shy of the threshold, lying flat on his side.

Ho, Peabody, what's up? Weren't you just here last week?

Mrs. Peabody, who was wearing those fancy kind of lady-dress-up shoes with a shiny bracelet around her ankle, pulled on the leash. "Come on, Snuggles, let's get better, shall we?" She waved a hand in front of her face. "Whew. Please, let's get better!"

I don' wanna go inside. I'm gassy.

MomDoc can't help you out here. Ya gotta go in. And besides, didn't we talk about you not getting into the trash anymore?

I know. I know.

Sheesh . . .

It took two people to lift Peabody to his feet and push him through the door. They shuffled him to the far corner of the waiting room near an open window.

"Stay here," Smith said. She was MomDoc's tech and was very familiar with the Peabody issue. "We'll come get him as soon as a room is available."

Peabody lay on his belly and covered his face with a paw.

I don' wan anyone to know it's me. . . .

It wasn't his face that people recognized, but I didn't say anything. He felt bad enough. Besides, there were lots more friends coming in. The place was hopping!

By the time MomDoc called me to the office for lunch, we'd seen dogs and cats, bunnies and chinchillas, even a turtle with blisters on his feet. Ozzie was spinning in circles, beside himself that he'd been stuck behind the gate on such an exciting morning.

"Calm down, silly," MomDoc said. "You're going to get dizzy!"

She opened her lunch and gave him a slice of pickle from

her sandwich. He scarfed it down in one gulp.

Burp.

Then he got right up close to me and panted pickle-breath in my face.

So, who was out there?

What happened?

Did everyone get better?

What was that smell?

MomDoc handed me a doggie cookie and I settled onto my office-bed with it. Ozzie and I each have beds in the clinic office, plus in the kitchen at home, in the living room, and upstairs in MomDoc's room. It's a lot of beds. My office-bed always had little crumbs from treats stuck down in the seams because that's where I ate my lunch every day.

Give me a minute. I'm hungry.

Ozzie stood in front of me while I nibbled the edge of the cookie. It had been a long morning. I wasn't in a hurry to answer his questions. There would just be more.

Oof, you gets all the fun!

It was true, but part of my responsibility was being sure Ozzie knew he was important.

It's my job. Your job is to keep an eye on MomDoc. Be sure she's okay. I work the front, you work the back. We're a team, remember?

He thought about this for a second, then came over and licked my ear.

Yeah, I 'member. You 'n' me, Di, we're a team.

I was back out front in the afternoon, doing my thing, when Max came in dragging his adoption-kid behind him by the leash.

Big Max! How's the home trial going?

Max was a huge tail-wagger, emphasis on huge. Mountain dog mixed with who-knows-what. His tail alone probably weighed as much as Ozzie. He swung it side to side, thumping it against the wall.

Bump. Bump. Bump.

Okay, I guess. Much better than living all alone in that barn like before.

I sidled up next to him.

You pooping outside yet?

The tail sped up. Bump. Bump. Bump. Bump. Bump.

Yeah. Boy said I'm a good dog.

Excellent. Does he let you sleep on his bed?

Mom said soon.

Bump. Bump. Bump. Bump. Bump. Bump. Bump.

Nice to be in a real home at last, right?

Yeah, thanks fur settin' me up. But I gotta tell ya, there was a new guy at the shelter. Came right before I left. Bad energy.

A new guy?

Not like Mike. Mike is good. This guy, I dunno.

My belly squeezed tight. I didn't like the sound of a new guy not-like-Mike taking care of our shelter-friends.

I'll check him out.

I was trotting toward the back to ponder this news when another kid saw me moving around without The Spare.

"Hey! That dog only has three legs!"

Max turned to look at him. So did the two other dogs waiting for MomDoc. The receptionist looked up from her desk.

"Yeah, he knows," she said.

I mean, *right*?

"Watch this."

She put a doggie cookie on the counter, right near the edge so I could just see it peeking over. Now, I'm not a big dog, I'm medium, or medium-small, and I'm no spring chicken anymore. But I am adorable. That's what everyone says. Plus, I'm clever, as you've probably already figured out. But if you didn't know me, like this kid obviously didn't, what I did next might come as a surprise.

With one big push off my lone back leg, I jumped high enough to knock that cookie off the counter with my nose. I grabbed it off the floor, jumped again with it in my teeth into a handstand, and walked on my two front paws to the kid and laid the cookie by his feet. His eyes got bigger than my paw.

"Wow! Did you see that, Dad?"

Of course he did. Everyone in the room saw.

"Go, MahDi!"

"Show your stuff, buddy!"

Oh, pssshaaaw . . .

"Dad, when we get a dog, I want one with three legs!"

The receptionist smiled over the counter. "He's hot stuff, that one. But three-legged dogs are hard to come by."

"Where'd he come from?"

"From a shelter, where all the best dogs are found."

"Dad," he said, tugging on the father's shirt. "Can we go to the shelter and look at the dogs? Please?"

I'm pretty sure I sealed the deal with that trick because when the kid and his dad carried their blue parakeet back for MomDoc to check over, the dad smiled and gave me the cookie I'd left with the boy.

"Well done, young man. Keep up the good work."

Near the end of our day, I was sitting beside a crate with two tiny kittens inside, reassuring them that *adoption* was a good word. One kitty had long white hair and blue eyes. The other was short-haired, black and white with green eyes. Two sisters in for their new adoption checkup with MomDoc. This was their first time at the clinic. All they'd ever known before was the cat room at the shelter where they'd been born.

Those dogs that just left? Both adopted. Happy and safe.

The black-and-white kitty tapped the gate and meowed. The white kitty shrank away.

I promise. And your new family is the best.

The front door opened and a whiff of something pleasant and lovely floated through the air. Coconut shampoo and peppermints. That could only mean one thing.

Lilah!

Our neighbor, Mr. Crandle, stepped inside holding Lilah's leash with one hand and balancing himself on a walking stick with the other. He saw me across the room and winked.

"I wore my special bow tie today, MahDi," he said.

My belly did that little tickle-flip thing. Mr. Crandle was the only one who knew about my secret crush. Every time he brought Lilah to the clinic, he wore the same bow tie. White with red hearts on it.

Lilah looked over at me, her beautiful sable face shining, her dark eyes smoldering, her pert ears so intelligent, so—

Hello, MahDi.

My heart skipped a beat.

Had she just batted her lashes at me?

I quivered and waited for someone to help Mr. Crandle get settled into a chair, then I left the kittens and went to her, my fabulous ginger-colored tail held high behind me.

Hello, Lilah.

She lowered her head and sat down.

"Such a coquette you are," Mr. Crandle said. He gave each of us a peppermint from his pocket, then whispered to me, "The love of my life made me wait, too."

If I had pockets like humans do, I would have carried peppermints everywhere just so I could have them when I saw Lilah. But I don't have pockets. I have a super-sniffer instead. It's a trade-off I think.

I sank to the floor near her.

Why are you here?

We were to come last week for a checkup, but he didn't feel well.

I sniffed Mr. Crandle's shoe, then up around his ankle. Lilah looked at me, worried.

Do you smell it?

I do. I do.

What does it mean?

I mulled this over for a moment. There was something, but I didn't know the exact source. Human smells are trickier than dog smells, more complicated. This was a bit of a mystery.

Maybe he needs more boiled rice and chicken. That's what Ozzie gets when his tummy is off.

Lilah lay on her belly with her nose right by Mr. Crandle's shoe.

Perhaps.

She was so lovely with her long, silky black hair, her thick lashes, and that look of love and worry for Mr. Crandle. She still wore the sparkly red collar MomDoc had given her on that Christmas night when we delivered her to his home, right after his wife went over the Rainbow Bridge. I'd never seen a human turn from hopeless to happy so fast. It was the best match we ever made.

Everything will be okay.

She closed her eyes.

I hope so.

CHAPTER 2

The next afternoon, MomDoc and I left Ozzie behind so we could deliver flowers and a wooden box to Mrs. Comfort, who'd just lost her Chihuahua, Precious. Ozzie wasn't having it and tried to block the door so we couldn't leave.

Why don' I get to go?

Delivering flowers is solemn. That's too hard for you.

Oof! Wud if I promise to be salad?

Solemn. And no. You stay here and guard the house.

That helped. A little. He ran off and perched on the sofa in the living room to keep watch out the window. A few minutes later, MomDoc and I were pulling out of the driveway with the flowers and a box of ashes in the back of the car. Domino, our toothless, tailless, one-eyed cat was sitting upright beside Ozzie, watching us leave. That old cat didn't care one lick if we took him on errands or not, but he knew it bothered Ozzie. He was waiting for just the right moment to taunt him.

"Bye, guys!" MomDoc waved. "Be good!"

As soon as she wasn't looking anymore, Domino swatted Ozzie across the head, then jumped away from the window.

When we got to her house, Mrs. Comfort was sitting squished into a chair in her living room, holding a bag of salmon dog treats, a picture of her dear, departed Precious— who MomDoc had helped find her way over the Rainbow Bridge a few days before—and a faded blanket that stank so bad I could practically taste the fluid that had turned the thing yellow.

"I know my Precious is better off." Mrs. Comfort sniffed. "She hurt so terribly at the end, not to mention her problem with widdling inside."

MomDoc handed her a tissue from a box on the table. "Precious was seventeen years old. That's a good long life for a Chihuahua. You did everything right."

In my opinion, Chihuahua's are too darn sassy to die young. Precious was no exception. Mrs. Comfort dabbed at her eyes.

"You were so good to her. She never liked our old vet."

I brushed myself lightly against her leg and tilted my head that way people always said made me look like a cute baby fox, hoping for a nibble of salmon jerky. But she just held that bag closer to her ample chest as if Precious might look down from The Great Beyond and wonder why one of those delicacies was missing. Precious was not inclined to share anything while she was alive, so I could see where Mrs. Comfort might think she wouldn't appreciate her giving me some salmon jerky even after she was gone.

MomDoc motioned to me that we were leaving and stuck a card into a basket of daisies she'd left on the table next to the wooden box of ashes.

"If you start feeling lonely, there's a cute little white dog at the shelter, about yea big," she said, spreading her hands out in front of her. "Lap-sized. I could bring her for a trial. She's older, very quiet, and her fur is soft and curly. When you're ready. Give yourself some time to grieve, of course. I understand."

Mrs. Comfort held the photo up in front of her face like she was trying to see if her dearly departed thought that would be a good idea. Apparently, Precious never answered because Mrs. Comfort was still staring at the picture when MomDoc and I slipped out the front door. When we got into the car, MomDoc kissed me right between the eyes.

"If I brought the little white dog over soon, do you think Mrs. Comfort would fall in love with her?"

I tucked my chin onto her arm.

Yes, yes, I do.

When we got home, a real, live Ozzie-disaster was in full throttle. Something had him totally worked up. He was jumping from one side of the sofa back to the other, barking and yipping frantically.

Nonstop.

High-pitched.

Annoying.

So loud we could hear him from inside the car—with the windows rolled up.

Alert! Alert! Chatty squirrel on the premises!

MomDoc braked and jumped out. She glanced next door to the house where a new lady had moved in. A grumpy new lady. With a baby.

"Ozzie! Quiet!"

Too late. The lady flung her door open and thrust her hands onto her hips. Her face puckered like it might if she stepped in something she didn't want to step in. The baby was crying inside.

"He's been barking for over an hour," she said. Her hair sprang in bunches all over her head like an unclipped, apricot-colored poodle.

"I'm sorry, Lydia," MomDoc said. "We were delivering flo—"

Lydia slammed the door shut before she even finished. I did not like people talking to MomDoc that way. That lady had been prickly ever since she moved in. I trotted toward her yard and let a small growl rumble in my throat.

Don't you even . . .

MomDoc snapped her fingers. "MahDi, get back here. That's not going to help."

Whatever.

I stopped at a wooden planter full of flowers on the sidewalk and left it dripping wet.

As soon as MomDoc opened the door, Ozzie bolted out so fast he crashed into me and knocked us both flat. Then he jumped up and sniffed me from head to tail.

Where've you been?

Who'd you see?

What did you do?

Why didn't I get to go?

One quick air-nip from me and he stood back.

You know where we were. Delivering flowers.

Oh yeah. Hey! There was a squirrel intruder!

He disappeared under the peony bushes and stuck his nose to the ground, dirt flying out behind him. The squirrel's scent was everywhere.

"Come inside, guys," MomDoc said. The peonies shook, but Ozzie didn't show his face. "If you come now, we'll go for a bike ride."

That got him. He poked his head out and shook faded pink flower petals from his face.

I'm in!

Then he scrambled ahead of us into the house, leaving a trail of dirt from the front door to the back. MomDoc shook her head and laughed.

"He's a mess, Di, isn't he?"

Yup. Sure is.

I trotted inside behind her.

CHAPTER 3

A few minutes later, we were out on the street with Ozzie running circles around MomDoc's bike.

We goin' to the butte?

MomDoc smiled down at him. "I know what you're thinking. You want to go to the butte, right?"

The butte! The butte!

And he was off.

A butte is like a small, steep mountain with a flat top. Ours has a switchback trail that weaves side to side all the way up. The path leading to it started at the opposite end of our road between two houses. One of them, the yellow house with the front porch swing, was where Lilah lived. On lucky days, Mr.

Crandle might be sitting on that porch swing, enjoying some fresh air and a glass of something cool to drink, with Lilah beside him. I ran along quickly and stopped by the yard, hoping to catch a glimpse of her if they happened to be outside. No such luck. Not this time. Even the windows were dark.

I trotted on between the houses, past clusters of aspen trees bordering the path, through some woods, and over a wooden bridge with the creek running underneath it. Around the next bend was the base of the butte where MomDoc and Ozzie were waiting for me. They loved hiking up that butte. Not me, not anymore. Once Ozzie came along, I let him go with MomDoc alone. Now I stay behind. Sniff things out. See who's been coming and going and get the news if anyone else was out for a walk.

MomDoc leaned her bike against a tree and gave me a treat from her pocket. "Be good, MahDi. We'll see you when we get back."

MomDoc and Ozzie couldn't have gotten very far when our kid neighbor, Toby, came around the bend gripping a leash with both hands and leaning back against the pull of an enormous dog at the other end.

"Hold on, Moose. Don't go so fast!"

I wasn't exactly sure how much Toby could see because his thick dark hair had fallen over his forehead and into his eyes. He was trying to dig his heels into the ground to stop, but that dog was nearly as big as a Shetland pony, hairy as a

Persian cat, with a tongue that hung almost to the ground, and only one thing on his mind. He was dragging Toby straight to the creek at the bottom of the hill. Nothing was going to keep him from that cool water.

"Stop!" Toby yelled.

I ran along beside the dog, barking and trying to get him to stop, but it didn't make a difference. Neither did Toby's pleading. Moose plunged ahead off the path and loped down the grassy hill, jerking Toby along behind him. At the bottom, they both went sailing off the bank and splashed into the water, landing smack in the middle of the creek.

I'm not a fan of swimming so I didn't jump in to save Toby, but I did run back and forth along the water's edge, barking and scolding the dog.

Bad Moose! Don't hurt him!

Toby stood up, soaked through and laughing. He wiped streams of water off his face and pushed his hair away, then reached down and patted Moose on the head.

"I kinda wanted to go swimming today, but not exactly like this."

Moose lapped water with that big tongue, making all kinds of funny gurgling sounds. After a full-body dunk he stood up and shook, spewing droplets from one side of the creek to the other, and all over Toby.

"Come on, out of the water," Toby said, pulling on the leash. "We need to get dry before I take you back to the shelter or no one will let me take you out again."

He tugged the giant dog up the hill from the creek. I trotted along beside them, watching the way Moose's paws left indents in the grass nearly the size of my dinner bowl at home. This was definitely one of the bigger dogs I'd ever seen, and there had been plenty. Moose lumbered through the grass, then plunked down and stretched out across the path in the sun and promptly fell asleep.

Toby took off his sneakers and dumped water out of them, then sat on a large rock along the edge of the trail and squeezed more creek water from his wet shirt.

"MahDi, you ever see a dog this big?"

I tilted my head and looked right at Toby. It was the only way I could answer since I didn't speak human. He reached out and scratched me behind my ear.

"When I get my dog, I don't think I want one that will eat as much as this guy because I have to earn the money to pay for it."

Toby lived right next door and was so good with animals that MomDoc sometimes let him stay with me and Ozzie when she and Domino went on her overnight trips to visit her Auntie. That was also why MomDoc asked Mike to let him volunteer at the shelter, even though he was only thirteen. Because Toby's dad said if he volunteered all summer, he'd let him get a dog of his own.

❦ ❦ ❦

By the time MomDoc and Ozzie got back, Toby and Moose were mostly dry. Moose was making puttering sounds while he slept, and he was still blocking the path so anyone who wanted to get by had to step over him or go around. This didn't sit well with Ozzie. He sidled up to me.

Hey! Who is that? Wuts he doin'?

Moose groaned and moved his shoulder around on the ground to scratch.

Moose, from the shelter.

Ozzie sniffed the back of his oversized head.

Oh-my-dog, did you see his teef yet? Are they big?

A red squirrel darted across the path and disappeared into a thicket. Ozzie couldn't resist. He forgot Moose and the possibility of his big teeth to chase the poor thing up a tree where it chastised him from a branch.

Chitchitchitchitchit!

"Hey, Toby, who's this?" MomDoc asked.

Toby stood up. "Moose, from the shelter. Some of the other dogs were kind of scared 'cuz of his size, so I brought him out here for a walk instead of putting him in the play yard."

"That's a long walk managing a guy this big," MomDoc said, grinning. "Unless he was the one doing the managing. He take you into the creek?"

Toby's face turned a deeper color and he pushed his hair back. "Yeah, he was hot and a lot stronger than me."

"Moose is a great name," MomDoc said.

"Thanks, I named him. But the new guy at the shelter said people would think he was dumb with that name."

"Who is the new guy?"

"Huck. He's temporary just while Mike goes for his surgery thing. He doesn't know much, though. He made me muzzle Moose, then he tried to put this harness on all tangled and inside out. I had to fix it, otherwise Moose could have gotten away, and we had to cross the road."

"Huh. Sounds like a character, but knowing Mike, he'll be sure he's up to snuff before he turns things over to him. Hopefully he just needs to learn."

Toby shrugged. "Maybe, but he doesn't want to learn from a kid, that's for sure. He didn't like it when I said it was on wrong. I was really polite, but he called me a name."

MomDoc thrust her fists onto her hips. "He called you a name?"

"Yeah." Toby shifted from one foot to the other and looked at the ground. "But can you not say anything to Mike or my dad? I don't want them to think I can't do the job."

"Of course, it's our secret. We have to go to the shelter soon to get a dog for Mrs. Comfort. I'll check him out then." MomDoc smiled and put her hand on Toby's arm. "You're a good kid. I'm glad we are friends."

CHAPTER 4

Usually, when Ozzie steals a stuffed squirrel from my pile, I snatch it right back. Not because I really need all the toys to myself, but to remind him how things are supposed to be. I am in charge.

Earlier, he'd nicked a squirrel from the pile in our office at the clinic and stashed it under MomDoc's desk. I didn't give two hoots what he stole. I even pretended not to notice.

Pfffft. As if. I notice everything.

I didn't let on because right before MomDoc went into an exam room with my friend Story, she said if we got done in time we'd go to the shelter.

"It's a matchmaking day, MahDi. Mrs. Comfort will like

that little white dog, don't you think?"

Matchmaking is one of the most important things Mom-Doc and I do—pairing up people and animals like Lilah and Mr. Crandle, and Max and his adoption-trial family. It's good work. There are always shelter dogs looking for new families, and there are plenty of humans who need them. Sometimes they just don't know it.

Whenever we go to the shelter, I always work the kennel room first and check on the dogs to be sure everyone's okay. I was locked in a cage once upon a time, too, but not in a nice place like Mike's. He's in charge of our shelter and almost always, between him and me and MomDoc, we find just the right home for the rescues.

Ozzie kept bouncing around the office like he wanted me to snatch the toy squirrel away. He shook it in his mouth so hard that the stuffing spilled out, then he hid under the desk, eyeing me suspiciously with his chin resting on top of the mangled critter.

It's hard not to notice Ozzie. His bottom teeth stick out from under masses of frizzy brown-and-black hair, kind of like a picket fence smothered by a field of overgrown weeds. Sometimes, when I feel feisty, I tease him about those teeth. He tips his head to the side like he doesn't understand, waiting for me to tell him I'm only being silly. And I do tell him that—sometimes. Depends on just how feisty I'm feeling.

Right then, though, I had to stay put. I had to wait. Not

only so I was ready to go to the shelter, but also because of Story. They'd bring him out of the exam room soon and lay him on the table where the big machine would take pictures inside his body so MomDoc could tell the family what Story and I already knew.

He had tumors.

Everywhere.

OZZIE

Huff.

Puff.

Pant.

Pant.

Did MahDi notice? I think he noticed.

Maybe not. He's too busy watching what's going on with MomDoc out in the clinic.

I stole a stuffed squirrel from his pile. Don't tell. I gots to be careful and not slobber on it. MahDi hates slobber. Maybe if I don' slobber he won't know I nabbed it.

Just in case I'm goin' to sit on it under the desk, so he won't see.

What's MahDi looking at out there, anyway?

Why isn't he paying attention to me?

Don' he know I gots his squirrel?

Hey, that's Story out there with MomDoc!

Huff.

Puff.

Pant.

Pant.

Story! Story!

Story don' look happy.

I can make Story happy if he'll just look over here.

That's what I do the best!

Ooof!

He walked right past, didn't even see me jumpin' up and down.

He and MahDi shared some kind of look though.

Hey, what's wrong with me? Am I chopped liver?

I love that joke.

MomDoc doesn't give us chopped liver because she says it makes us *emit noxious fumes.*

I don' know what that means but she bunches her nose funny when she says it.

I love Story.

Not that greyhound, though, the one who came in before. She stopped right in front of me and MahDi and stretched her long legs one at a time.

Show-off.

Di only has three legs and mine are tiny-but-mighty. MomDoc calls them *mini-pistons.*

I tried eating a carrot once to make my legs grow long. It was awful and got stuck in my teef. MomDoc poked it out with a toofpick and it made my mouth bleed.

Not fun.

MomDoc says my teef are like the white picket fence that goes around the flower garden at home. A flower garden— not dead grass like MahDi says.

He's always teasing me.

People say *look how cute he is with those teef.*

Di has perfect teef.

Domino doesn't have any.

So long as people smile when they say it, I'm okay.

Sometimes Di says my hair is like a *rat's nest.*

Wuts that all about?

Just 'cuz his coat is golden and long and silky and his ears are perfect and people say he looks like a sweet baby fox.

Not much sweet about a fox if you ask me. They eat the neighbor's chickens.

I learned the hard way.

Do. Not. Go. Near. The. Chickens!

Sigh . . .

Even with the teasing, I know MahDi loves me.

Hey, he jumped up.

He's excited!

Wuts going on?

Who is here?

Where are we going?

The car! The car!

Oh boy! I'm goin' first!

Oh no! MahDi snatched my squirrel away!

Where?

Wha?

How?

Hey, MahDi, where are we goin'?

To the shelter to rescue another dog, Ozzie. Just like we did with you, and MomDoc did with me.

CHAPTER 5

MomDoc reached over and put her hand on my back where I was sitting in the front seat of the car.

"It's okay, MahDi."

As soon as she said that I knew the white truck was at the shelter again. I peered out the car window and sure enough, there it was, passing so close I imagined I could smell the dogs inside. I dropped down and closed my eyes, pressing my whole body against the seat and shaking so hard that Mom-Doc's hand jiggled.

"It's okay. That white truck isn't going to hurt you, I promise."

Usually, when we got in front of the shelter I was sitting

upright, poised and panting, ready to jump out. But whenever that big white truck showed up, it took a lot of coaxing to get me to budge. I was terrified of it.

"Come on, buddy," she said, opening her door. "Mike's outside and it looks like he has company. Must be the new guy. Let's go check him out."

Domino, who had snuck into the car unnoticed before we left, jumped from the back seat and bolted for the office with Ozzie yipping right behind him.

Treats! Treats!

Mike took care of all the animals in the shelter, but his wife, Rebecca, was the keeper of treats. She had a whole drawer full that she kept in the office just for us. Okay, so she gave them out to other dogs, too, but she saved the kinds we liked best in a secret place. Not plain biscuits. Real treats. Like jerky. But this time I stayed close to MomDoc. If something terrible and awful happened, like if that truck turned around and came back to snatch me away, she'd be right there to save me.

Again.

Mike was sitting on the porch steps of the shelter building, his elbows propped on his knees. He smiled when he saw me cowering by MomDoc's leg and put out a hand.

"Hey, MahDi. You okay, buddy?"

"He's still scared of white trucks," MomDoc said. "Has been since before my time. Why was it here?"

She was only partially right.

I *was* still scared of white trucks.

But there was something else. The guy sitting next to Mike.

I didn't like him.

And he didn't like me, either.

"Nothing bad," Mike said. "Just transporting a dog to another shelter where they have a home lined up."

The new guy's tiny black eyes darted between me and MomDoc. He had dark circles under his armpits and smelled rank, like rotten food. He shoved a stack of potato chips into his mouth from a can. Mike nodded toward him.

"Doc, this is Huck. He's going to be here as a temp while I'm off for my surgery."

Huck wiped his mouth with the back of his hand, then stuck it out for MomDoc to shake. That's what humans do when they first meet each other, which is the same as when dog's sniff each other's rear ends—only not. To my knowledge, humans don't sniff rear ends.

"Nice to meet you," MomDoc said. "You here from another shelter?"

"Pffft, naw," he said. He puffed out his chest and slapped his hands on his thighs. "I'm gonna be a cop, but training don't start until October and I still gotta pay the rent, so the recruiter gave me a list of temp jobs."

MomDoc's eyebrows stitched together and she studied

Huck's face. "Ah, well, welcome. So, Mike, when is the surgery again?"

"Ten days from now," Mike said. "Huck's here a little early to get some training before I hand him the keys."

Huck jerked his thumb at me. "Who's that?"

Mike smiled at me the way that always made me feel warm inside.

"That," he said, "is the best canine partner you'll ever see. MahDi works with Doc at the vet clinic and checks on the newbies here at the shelter, makes sure they feel safe."

Huck scoffed. "Huh, you talk about that dog like he knows what's up."

The hair raised on the back of my neck. Of course I know what's up!

"Yes, well, you'll see," MomDoc said. A tiny smile flickered on her face.

Mike pulled a doggie treat from his shirt pocket and held it out for me. "Doc and I have been working together ever since she got out of vet school. What's that been now, fifteen years?"

"Something like that, yeah."

Huck shook the chip can and peered inside, like he was studying them. Ozzie had a sniffer that could detect a potato chip from the top of the butte to the bottom. He flew back out the door and ran toward the smell, spinning around MomDoc's legs, then skidded to a stop, eyeing Huck, then the can, then Huck again. Instead of diving to snatch a chip, he pivoted toward me and tucked his tail.

Oh-my-dog, never trust someone who eats 'em from a can.

Huck clutched the can tighter and pulled his hands up close to his chest, just like Mrs. Comfort had done with that bag of salmon dog treats. Only not like her, because Huck pinned those beady little eyes on Ozzie and made his lips bunch up all tight. Mrs. Comfort did it because she was sad about losing Precious. Huck did it because he was afraid.

Ozzie revved up his little mini-piston legs and bolted for the office.

I'm outta here!

I made a wide circle around Huck and Mike and followed him inside, where the familiar smells of the office made me feel more settled right away. Dogs, cats, coffee, people, kids, the guy who delivered dog food, and Toby.

"Well, hello, MahDi. I was wondering when you'd come see me," Rebecca said. She was perched on the edge of the desk stroking Domino, who had made himself at home across the top and was purring loudly. "Did Ozzie tell you I have new treats today?"

Rebecca always smelled a little bit like Mike, a little bit like soap, and a lot like dog and cat treats. Especially the tips of her fingers. Ozzie stood by her chair gazing up at her, his head tilted and his little tail wagging.

New treats! New treats!

"Oh, you are so cute, I can never resist!"

She opened the secret drawer, took out a bag, and shook it.

"Guess what kind?"

Ozzie whirled around chasing his tail, dropped down, and rolled onto his back with his legs stuck straight up, then jumped onto Rebecca's chair and pushed the edge of the desk with his nose to make the chair spin. Rebecca grabbed the back of the chair to make it stop and laughed.

"You and your antics, Ozzie. You've earned at least a dozen already, my sweet little puppet."

Ozzie snatched his treat so fast I barely had time to detect what it was before he'd swallowed it whole. But I did get a whiff. Fish skins. One of our all-time faves.

"Here you go, MahDi."

I took the crunchy bit, then trotted to the door to the kennel room and waited for Rebecca to open it for me.

"You go make your rounds, Di. Ozzie and Domino and I will be right here."

It was time for me to go to work.

The dog part of the shelter was set up in one long room with chain-link kennels, five on each side of a wide aisle running down the middle. Each pen had a gate in the front and a door in the back to private yards, so the dogs could go outside to relieve themselves whenever they wanted. At the very end of the aisle was another set of doors that went to a big fenced-in grassy area where Toby took groups of dogs out for exercise and to play together.

Sometimes Mike had too many dogs and not enough people to adopt them. When that happened, he doubled them up in the pens and kept the smaller dogs in crates stacked on top of each other down at the end. Those stacked crates reminded me of my life before MomDoc and the terrible, awful thing that happened. It didn't get crowded at our shelter very often, though, because Mike and MomDoc worked really hard to get our shelter-friends adopted by new families.

I went straight to the first kennel, where a shepherd-type dog named Leroi lived. Mike never put extras in with her. Not because she would fight, but because she was a *long-timer*. Leroi had her own person called Murph and didn't need to be adopted by a new family. She just needed Murph to come home from the hospital.

Leroi thumped her tail against the ground when she saw me.

Murph okay?

She came to the gate so we could sniff, then sat down on her side and looked at me with yellow eyes.

Happy today.

Murph called Mike on the phone every week so Leroi could hear him talk to her. If Murph sounded happy, Leroi was content. When he didn't sound happy, Leroi got agitated and wouldn't eat.

Happy is good.

He said maybe soon he will come for me.

I made my way down the aisle toward the end where the little white dog had been the last time we were here. Some of the kennels were empty, which meant Toby might have some of the shelter-friends out in the play yard. I stopped at all the others to check in.

Moose! You're still here!

Moose looked up without raising his head. His eyelids were rimmed in red.

Is there 'nuther place you think I should be?

He closed his eyes and puttering noises bubbled from his mouth.

A few doors down, I stopped to see Tootsie, a pale, curly-haired dog with a little bit of a limp.

How's it goin', Toots?

Mike had named Tootsie because he said she looked like someone wearing a wig that was too big for her. Tootsie said the name made her feel glamorous.

Look at my nails! Just like a movie star!

Dogs can't see color the same way humans do, but Tootsie's nails were darker with tiny bits of something shiny on them.

What color?

Christmas Red, she said.

Nice. Christmas Red sounds merry.

Tootsie lay on her belly with her front paws stretched out so she could stare at her newly painted glamour nails. Her eyes shined.

Yes, merry. I like that. I think I'll get adopted faster now, don't you?

If all it took was painting a dog's nails for them to be snatched up, my job wouldn't exist. It didn't work quite like that, but I didn't tell her.

Of course, Toots. I think so, too.

I went on to the last kennel to see Mrs. Comfort's dog, but it was empty. An orange tag hung limply from the gate. There hadn't been an orange tag on a kennel for a very long time. It made my belly hurt, just seeing it there now. A long time ago, those orange tags used to mean the dog had been at the shelter too long without getting adopted and had to go to the back room for The Unthinkable. Mike said that every single time he had to take a dog back there, he cried. Rebecca said every single time he had bad dreams that night. But the door to that room where The Unthinkable happened had been closed for a long, long time.

MomDoc and I had found Ozzie in an orange tag kennel several years back. Someone had discarded him in the nighttime drop pen outside, and by the time we saw him, no one had adopted him. He was scheduled for The Unthinkable the very next day.

No, I'm not going to tell you what The Unthinkable means. It's unthinkable and you don't want to know.

As soon as I saw Ozzie that first time, standing with his front paws braced against the gate, and his whole little body with all that dark curly hair wiggling with joy for absolutely no reason at all, I knew he was meant to come home with us. MomDoc saw the orange tag, read his information card, and opened his gate.

"Come on, you're coming with us!"

The two of us ran side by side to the car as if he'd been part of our family forever. On the drive home MomDoc laughed at us playing in the back seat.

"You two fit together like kibbles and gravy."

Ozzie was the best save ever.

Well, him and Lilah both.

Matchmaking was good and important work. But now the white dog was gone and there was an orange tag. I didn't like the way any of this felt.

CHAPTER 6

The door near the office swung open and MomDoc strode toward me with a leash in one hand and her vet bag in the other. Mike followed close behind her with Huck on his heels. When MomDoc saw the kennel gate propped open and the orange tag still hanging from the front, she stopped short, then swung around to face Mike.

"Where's that little white dog?"

"That's the one who was transported to the other shelter."

"Oh, gotcha," MomDoc said. Her shoulders relaxed. "But darn, I was going to take that dog to my neighbor."

"I'm really sorry, you should have called me. I would have pulled her, but the county's breathing down my neck. I've been calling all these other shelters looking for homes for all the extra dogs coming in."

"What's the orange tag doing there?"

Mike looked behind himself quickly. Huck had gone back to the office and no one else was there. "The policies and procedures book says those tags are used for dogs who've been here too long. Huck's been reading that book cover to cover."

MomDoc wrinkled her nose. "Does he think we euthanize dogs here?"

"He knows we don't," Mike said. "But he thinks we should, since those are the official guidelines. He's all about the rules."

MomDoc hoisted her vet bag up on the inspection table at the end of the aisle. "Well, it's really none of his business, right? Anyway, let me see the dog with the cut ear you called about."

Mike brought a little Jack Russell terrier out of a kennel and put her on the vet table.

"Where'd that guy go?" MomDoc asked.

Mike shook his head and grinned. "In the office, I bet. Seems to think this is a desk job. I'm not telling him. Hard to find help as it is, but especially temps. I'm just easing him into the real work."

MomDoc peered closely at the dog's ear. "The cut is clean, a few stitches will take care of it."

I sat nearby while she took out her cut-fixing equipment

and went to work. She was just tying off the stitches when Huck came in from the office.

"That other dog you brought with you is noisy," he complained. "Doesn't stay still for a second."

MomDoc glanced up. "That would be Ozzie and yes, he's a little spitfire."

Huck looked away and narrowed his eyes at me. He stank fishy, but not fishy like treats. Fishy like what he showed on the outside wasn't what was lurking inside his heart. And besides, anyone who didn't like Ozzie had something wrong with them. I can't even tell you how badly I wanted to use his leg for a tree. But I didn't. Because MomDoc wouldn't want me to.

Toby came in from the play yard with five other dogs, all yipping and barking and pulling on their leashes.

"Hey, slow down everyone!" he yelled.

The Jack Russell startled at the noise, jerked loose from Mike's grasp, and fell against Huck's chest. Huck's hands flew out and he shoved her across the table.

"Ah! Get away!"

"Whoa, whoa, whoa!" Mike grabbed the dog and cradled her against himself. "Calm down, Huck. She's not trying to hurt you!"

Huck's eyes darted between MomDoc and Mike. "Sorry, it surprised me, that's all. Sorry, sorry. Come here, little pooch."

He reached out to try to pet her, but the terrier cowered

and raised her lip. Huck snatched his hand away. Only smart thing I'd seen him do yet.

"Why don't you go on back to the office for now while we finish up here, okay?" Mike said.

"Okay by me." And off he went.

Toby got all the dogs back in their kennels and came over, his face flushed. "Sorry about that. I guess I tried to bring too many in at the same time."

"No worries," Mike said. He lifted the dog from the table and ran his hands gently over her trembling body. "It's okay, tiny girl. Back to bed for you until that heals a little."

After Mike walked away, Toby turned to MomDoc. "That's the guy I was telling you about. The one who put the harness on Moose all wrong and called me a name."

"Oh yeah, I thought it must be. Mike will set him right."

But Toby was still upset. I sat down on top of his foot and pressed my head against his leg. That usually helped, but not so much this time.

"He put the orange tag on that kennel, even though Mike told him the dog was just being transported."

Mike came back from getting the terrier settled. "I told him we are a no-kill shelter now. You can take the tag off."

I followed Toby to the end of the aisle. When he cut off the tag, it fell to the floor. I picked that thing up and carried it out the back door to the play yard and shoved it through the fence toward the street.

Take that!

That's when it hit me. Tootsie! For Mrs. Comfort! She would be perfect! I ran to her kennel and spun around, waiting for MomDoc to notice me. When she didn't, I had to resort to howling.

Raruuuu!

Toby understood me right away.

"Hey, Doc, are you still looking for a dog for Mrs. Comfort?"

Tootsie stretched out her paws to show them her fancy nails.

Oh, pick me! Please pick me!

MomDoc looked into Tootsie's pen and smiled. "Well, she's not what I described, but Mrs. Comfort does love a fancy dog. Let me call her."

She got her phone out and within a few minutes it was all settled. Tootsie would go to Mrs. Comfort's house for a trial. And she would be living so close by!

"Let's give her a quick bath and spruce her up," MomDoc said. "I'll get a ribbon from Rebecca. Mrs. Comfort will go crazy for those nails, too."

When she was all prettied up, Tootsie asked me if she looked like a movie star. I'd never seen a movie star, but her pale hair was soft and wavy with a wisp of curls tied on the top of her head with a piece of ribbon.

The most beautiful movie star ever.

She pranced like a parade pony out the door when we left,

fancy enough to capture Mrs. Comfort's heart.

Huck was sitting in Rebecca's chair when we went through the office.

"One less dog for you to worry about, Huck," Mike said.

Huck stuck his thumb up in the air and grinned. "Even better."

"Okay, everyone, out to the car," MomDoc said.

Huck glared at us as we ran past. Ozzie and I kept our distance from him. We knew he didn't want us near him and that was just fine. Domino was a different story. He didn't like Huck any better than any of us, but he wasn't going to just walk past. We were waiting for MomDoc on the front porch when we heard a loud screech and a hiss, then a human squeal. Domino darted out the door and jumped from the porch steps all the way through the open car window into the back seat.

Huck hobbled outside, his face dark, holding a hand over the lower part of his leg. "That ugly cat scratched me!"

MomDoc came out behind him, keys in hand. "Animals can sense things a lot better than humans," she said. "I would be careful about calling Domino ugly."

She climbed into her seat and shook her finger at Domino.

"I suspect you might have had reason to not like him, but you know we don't scratch people."

Domino just blinked his one eye and licked a paw.

Wanna bet?

❧ ❧ ❧

Mrs. Comfort loved Tootsie right away. "Come, come, let's go outside for a quick widdle," she said.

Tootsie did her business, then Mrs. Comfort settled into her big chair. "Up, now, and let me see those fancy nails of yours."

Tootsie jumped into her lap and put one paw on the arm of the chair.

"Oh, aren't you the smart one, and so glamorous!" She ran the tip of her finger over the nails and smiled. "I have a drawer full of different-colored polish. Precious only liked pink, but I think you will like them all."

Tootsie had been right. Her pretty nails had gotten her a new home. If all it took was a bit of polish for every dog to find the perfect family, I'd be out of a job and that white truck would never show up again.

LEROI

Mike pulls the rope that makes the door in the back of my kennel slide open so I can go out to my private yard.

"Don't be long. Murph's gonna call today!"

I trot out into the sunshine. Yesterday was dark with rain. Today is sunshine. I never know what kind of day it will be until it is here. The same way I never know which Murph will call until Mike holds the phone up for me to listen to his voice.

Murph and I used to live in a house together, but then sunshine-Murph turned into stormy-Murph, which is why he is where he is, and I am where I am.

For now.

At the far end of my yard, I relieve myself by the wooden bucket of flowers. I am the only dog here who has plants growing inside their pen, but I am also the only dog who stays this long. I'm an *exception*. That's what Mike calls it.

Sometimes I go home with Mike and Rebecca for a few days, and I've even stayed over at Doc's with MahDi and Ozzie and that wicked-smart cat, Domino. Lots of dogs go on adoption trials with other people, but I only go with Mike or Doc. No strangers are allowed to keep me because I'm waiting for Murph to come home.

The house Murph and I lived in didn't have plants or flowers. Sometimes the roof leaked when it rained and he'd pull a piece of plastic over us on the couch. I didn't mind that kind of storm, the kind with rain that came from outside. It was the storm inside Murph that frightened me. It's not bad being here at Mike's shelter, but it's been too long now. I'm ready to go back to the house with outside rain.

When Mike brings the phone for me to hear Murph talk, he is smiling. That means Murph is having a good day. No storm. Mike comes inside my kennel, sits on the floor, and leans his back against the wall. He punches a button on the phone, then says, "Okay, Murph, she can hear you now!"

I sit up, alert, and listen to Murph's voice. It sounds tiny, far away, not like when Murph is beside me, but he talks, then laughs, then talks some more and says, "Good girl!" a lot. I lick the phone and my tail thumps against the floor. I am happy.

I was only a pup when Murph found me inside a cardboard box next to a highway and named me Leroi. Later, he said Leroi is a boy name and since I am a girl he could change it if I wanted. I didn't answer, so he kept calling me Leroi.

"Bye, Leroi, bye. I'll see you really soon, I think!"

Mike smiles and puts the phone away. "He sounded good, don't you think?"

I ache for the day when Murph and I can be together again, but until he's better, I'm okay. I have my plants and blankets and visits to Doc's or Mike's houses, and Murph knows where I am. I get fed twice a day now, which didn't always happen before. Sometimes we'd run out of food, but then Murph learned we could get it for free at Doc's clinic. They didn't have food for Murph. I tried to share but he said, *No, you eat, I'm okay*, even though I knew he was often hungry.

When the storm took over and Murph went away, he left me at Doc's clinic because he knew I'd be safe until he got well and came home. I stretch out on my blanket and let the warm sunshine lull me almost to sleep until some people come to see about adopting a dog and someone gets loose and everyone gets all excited and loud.

Sometimes it's so noisy here I have to put my paws over my ears so they don't break.

CHAPTER 7

A few evenings after Huck started at the shelter, I was lying across the round back of the sofa in the front window when our neighbor Jimmy limped up the walkway and rang the bell. Jimmy's legs were shaped like a bowl. He was the only human I'd ever seen wobble side to side and move forward at the same time.

"It's because he used to be a rodeo clown," MomDoc had said.

I don't know anything about rodeo clowns except that Jimmy liked to play a game in the street with the other 'hood dogs called Rodeo, where he waved a red cloth in the air and all the dogs jumped and barked and leaped and tumbled, pushing each other down trying to be the one who got the flag out of his hand. Which was exactly why I only watched and didn't play. Three legs, remember?

MomDoc opened the door. "Oh, hello, neighbor."

Jimmy twisted the red cloth in his hands. "Anyone for a game of Rodeo?"

"I'm sure Ozzie would love it."

Ozzie raced down the stairs and sped past the two of them, his ears flying and a white sock from the laundry basket stuck to his back.

Rodeo! Rodeo!

He skidded to a stop in the yard beside his friend Chloe. The two of them sniffed and wagged their tails, hers blond and feathery, his dark and kinky. Then they ran off together to round up the 'hood pack and let them know Jimmy was out to play.

"Say, before I get started with the dogs," Jimmy said, "I wanted to talk to you about Bullseye."

"Not right now, Jimmy. I'm working on a proposal to help Mike get the new shelter rules changed. Can we talk later?"

"Oh, sure. Wait, what rules?"

"The shelter's been overrun with dogs, so Mike's been transporting them out when he can't find homes here. It used to be that dogs who didn't get adopted quickly were disposed of. That could happen again if we can't get some support."

I gnawed at the top of a paw.

Jimmy pinched the space between his eyes. "What does that mean, disposed of?"

MomDoc put her hands on her hips. "Jimmy, you know exactly what I mean. We need homes, which is why I keep trying to get you to move on from Bullseye. It's been five years since Mary and Bullseye left. There are so many great dogs looking for homes, I'm not sure how to convince you it's the right thing to do."

From outside, the familiar sound of skateboards rumbled up the street. Toby's friend from another 'hood soared over the hill next to his beagle. The two of them whizzed past, each riding their own skateboards, the beagle's ears flying behind him.

"Now see," Jimmy said. "If I could find a dog like that, a dog that knows how to do clever things, well, I might consider it. Then Bullseye might understand if he and Mary ever come home."

MomDoc smiled and patted Jimmy's arm. "Well, that's just great because that dog on the skateboard was a rescue from our shelter. I can find you one just like him if you want."

Jimmy put his hand against his chest. "I'll keep that in mind, Doc, but my old heart, ya know. It hurt real bad after Bullseye."

Outside, Ozzie and Chloe tumbled around in the grass. Chloe tugged on Ozzie's ear and he rolled away, pretending to be hurt so she'd get up close to comfort him. Then he jumped up and ran off barking, *Catch me!*

Daisy, the blue Frenchie who lived on the other side of Jimmy, trotted up the sidewalk flanked by her black and yellow Lab henchmen, Jaws and Luther. Her family's granddaughter must have been visiting because a hot-pink tutu was stretched around Daisy's waist, and shimmering tulle waved side to side in the sun. Poor Daisy would have to wear that thing every day until the granddaughter left. Then she'd have another rash from the elastic and end up at the clinic again. But nothing would keep her from a game of Rodeo.

Peabody lumbered over and sprawled out in the shade of an azalea bush. Ozzie sniffed his rear end, then ran off.

Stay clear! Stay clear!

If only Mrs. Peabody would get one of the trash cans with a lid, his gas problem could go away.

Pilot, a black-and-white border collie mix with an appetite for herding, jumped her fence when she saw everyone gathering in our yard and ran down the street. She made circles around the 'hood dogs and started nipping them from behind until they were all in a tight bunch. She even got Peabody up on his feet before Jimmy stepped out.

"Whooooo's ready? Who wants to play Roe-Dae-Oh?"

He flipped the flag around in the air until Ozzie and Chloe and Daisy were jumping and spinning around his legs. Jaws and Luther trailed along behind Daisy, and even old Peabody, with his floppy ears and fat body, plodded around with the rest of the 'hood pack like he thought there might be a universe in which he was quick enough to get that piece of cloth.

Oh, Peabody . . .

I rested my chin on my front paws and watched. MomDoc and I had rescued every one of those dogs and matched them with just the right homes. It was good work. But when they were all together in a pack, like when they played Rodeo in the street, it was hard not to remember the dogs I hadn't saved in my life before MomDoc, back when I was called Little-D. It was still too hard to think about.

LITTLE-D

The den I was born in sat deep in the woods by the roots of a very tall evergreen tree. Before my eyes ever opened, my super-sniffer knew the pungent smell of sap and dried leaves, the sounds of crows and vultures, and the soft fur and swollen belly of Mother. I was the smallest of six pups and not one of us looked alike. We slept curled together in our cozy home like a living, breathing puzzle.

Every day Mother left to get food. When she returned, her rough tongue cleaned us frantically, letting out a sharp breath that filled our space with the scent of strange, unrecognizable things from the places she traveled. We crawled across her belly and dug tiny toes into her sides, trying to reach the most milk. We relied on Mother for food and to keep us clean and safe, but on each other for company and warmth.

As we got older we explored the woods around our den, playing among the tall trees and venturing near the bottom of a long slope, where a wide, wandering stream moved across the ground like a snake. We followed Mother's scent to where the earth rose sharply up to a place that was noisy and frightening and busy.

I was the smallest but also the most adventurous, the first to climb the craggy hill and see the road with my own eyes. The first to glimpse two-legged humans and to feel the rush of wind when noisy, smelly cars roared past. I was drawn by the strangeness of what went on at the top of that hill. Each day I ventured closer, hiding in tall weeds beside the road, watching the people moving swiftly back and forth.

The noise was so constant I felt the rumble of a big white truck approaching before I actually saw it. The back was covered by a tarp tied down at the corners, but when it stopped, the edge of the tarp flipped up. Dozens of dogs were trapped inside crates, whimpering, barking, their eyes begging for help. The truck moved again and the dogs were carried away.

I stumbled down the hill and ran all the way to our den, still shaking when Mother came in and snapped at me.

Don't go there again! They catch bait.

Danger.

We didn't know what *bait* meant, but her warning was

serious. After that we only explored along the stream, away from the frightening road. When Mother found us bravely touching our paws to the water, she nipped us and herded us home.

Stay away. The river is dangerous. I will teach you.

But we were young and curious and didn't listen. Before long that river had reduced our litter to four. Brown-Eared Sister tumbled in and was carried away by a swift current, her little head bobbing beneath the surface while the rest of us ran along the bank, barking frantically. A few days later, Big Brother jumped from a rock after a fish and sank. He never returned.

After that, Mother left and did not come back. We never knew what called her away, we only knew that when she left that time, she didn't turn around to say goodbye.

And just like that, we were on our own.

Our first night alone we clung to each other, sad and confused, our bellies twisted with hunger.

Where is Mother?

Who will feed us?

What will we do?

In the morning we rallied and went in search of food, scouring the woods, but found nothing. We went back to our den hungry, tired, and sore. The next day, weak but driven by vacant bellies, we scrambled up the hill to the road. Taunted by the scent of cooked meat, we stumbled through the tall grass alongside busy streets that crossed this way and that. We skirted down dirty alleys and past strange dogs digging through trash spilled from a bin. I gnawed a discarded paper bag stained with grease while Clumsy Brother snatched the spine of a fish and loped away.

Somehow I got separated from the others and spent a lonely night waiting for them in our den. Little Sister stumbled in before daybreak, but the others were gone, caught up in a net and thrown into a cage on the back of a white truck.

Bait, Mother had said.

And then we were two.

We joined a pack of wise street dogs who scavenged for food by day and slept in the woods at night. Because we were young, after a bit of scuffling to show us who was alpha and who was not, they accepted us and helped us learn how to survive on our own.

> *Stay together.*
>
> *Don't get caught in the nets.*
>
> *Beware of strangers.*

Little Sis and I were bound by fear and an instinct to survive, searching always for food. We spent our nights curled up together in a ragged basket behind some shops, keeping warm and hoping for a glimpse of Mother.

One day we followed the pack down a long, dusty road to a building that stood by itself and was surrounded by trees. We sat near the road with the others, waiting, until a group of children came outside. It was frightening at first; the small humans were quite noisy. They sat under the trees and held out pieces of bread for us. The wiser street dogs went confidently to them and ate from their hands. Little Sis and I watched from a distance. One boy saw us and smiled, waving a piece of bread in his hand.

"Don't be afraid," he said. "Come eat."

His voice was soothing. We went to him, slowly at first, then we ran and snatched the food and ate. My first experience with humans was when that boy gently untangled the hair matted behind my ears while I scarfed down a large chunk of crusty bread.

"You are cute," he said.

I didn't know what the words meant, but I was comforted by his touch, the tone of his voice, and the food he gave me until I was full. When we couldn't find enough to eat on the streets, we went back to that building and waited for the children to come outside and share their meal. Eventually, Little Sis paired up with a male dog who protected her and went off, leaving me alone with my street pack. Thoughts of finding Mother faded away.

I lived this way and grew strong and confident as I ran through the streets near the shops, stealing discarded meat from trash cans and anything else I could find, or going to the building with all the children to see the boy. Before long I thought of him as "mine" and often went alone, sitting beside him when I ate. I let him brush my coat with his fingers and from time to time he pulled me into his lap and kissed the top of my head.

"I wish I could take you home," he said. "I'm Derrick. I'm calling you Little-D."

Sometimes another stray dog would come up, begging for some of my food, but I'd snap at them and send them away.

Get your own boy.

Over time, a little pack of stray dogs formed with me as the leader. We cruised the streets together looking for scraps to share, and played in the yard by the building, sleeping in the shade while we waited for the children to come out and feed us. One time, a few of us went deeper into the woods to hunt, frolicking carelessly under the trees beside a small lake. We never saw the net fall from the branches above us until we were trapped. We flailed wildly, desperate to claw our way out, but men descended and worked quickly, reaching under the net, grabbing us by the scruff of our necks and locking us in wooden crates that they then shoved onto the back of a truck. We clawed at the sides of our prisons until our paws were bloody, but there was no way out.

We were doomed.

The crates were stacked on top of each other, so close there was no way to escape the smell of fear. At dark, the truck rumbled to life and lurched forward out of the woods.

We'd had no food and no water. Someone above me relieved himself in fear. Yellow liquid dribbled down and pooled in the fur on my back.

I didn't know why the truck lurched off the road, I only knew it was dark and suddenly the truck ricocheted off the side of a hill, the front end broke apart, and we spun and bounced and screamed, our fate tied together like the death traps we were in. The truck jolted and bounced, and when it landed hard, my back leg was thrust between two slats of wood and stuck outside the crate. Each time we hit a bump, the truck rose and fell, and the box on top of mine slammed down, pinning the boards tighter around my leg. Bit by bit, my leg was crushed. When the spinning stopped, we had landed at the bottom of the hill.

Silence.

It was a long while before anyone found us. They dug through the wreckage looking for survivors and when they discovered me breathing one of them shouted, "Alive!"

They broke open my crate, laid me on a blanket, and carried me away. Somehow, I had survived.

The others did not.

When I awoke, the lights were bright and hurt my eyes. Someone hovered over me, a human. Its face was covered partway with a piece of green fabric. The human made a noise, but I didn't understand because the mouth was behind that mask.

I didn't know words back then, anyway.

Sharp, bitter smells burned my nose. I closed my eyes and drifted back to sleep.

It wasn't a nice sleep.

It wasn't a dreamless sleep.

I dreamed endlessly about the dog who was crushed on top of me when the truck careened down the side of the hill. I dreamed about dogs being locked inside wire cages and wooden crates, and the heart-wrenching sound of whimpering. I dreamed of terror.

Some of the dogs I knew from my days living in a street pack.

Others were strangers.

We all wanted the same thing: to survive.

When I dreamed about my back leg hanging between the bars of the crate I was trapped in, I startled awake. The fabric-covered face was gone. And so was the leg.

A man leaned down close to me. A cigarette dangled from his mouth. White smoke curled into a spiral.

"It was just a spare," he said. He smiled with the cigarette still between his lips. "You'll be fine without it."

I fell back asleep, not understanding his words.

I learned his name was John. Every day he carried me to a small yard outside. There, he lowered me to the ground, holding up my back end with a cloth wrapped under my belly.

If he'd let go, I would have fallen.

"You'll learn to do this on your own soon enough," he said.

He waited for me to relieve myself, but peeing made me feel shy. I waited, hoping he would look the other way, but he held tight to the cloth with one hand and puffed his cigarette with the other.

"I can't let go, friend. You gotta get over that."

After my bandages came off, the doctor told John to move me back out with the others. "He'll be happier with company. He'll learn to get around on three legs."

I didn't like being with other dogs. Dozens of them cried and whined and barked all day. The noise reminded me of being trapped. There were dogs of all shapes, colors, and sizes, and occasionally I thought I caught a whiff of one who might be familiar. The others ran and played all day, sometimes fighting, then resting, then playing more. I didn't know where they'd come from, but I stayed in a corner by myself, waiting for John to bring me back inside.

One time, a new dog arrived who was determined to escape. He already knew how to climb the chain-link fence, and I watched him do it and run off into the woods surrounding the place. I didn't want to stay, either. I wanted to go back to the streets, away from the strange dogs, so I taught myself how to climb the fence with just three legs. Link by link, I scaled the wall until I got to the top and fell over.

John found me lying in the grass, my wound ripped open

and a piece of bone exposed. I went back into the clinic to heal, and when I was well enough and John put me out with the others, he'd run a line of hot wire across the fence. No dogs climbed out ever again.

One afternoon, John kept me inside and combed out my fur with a brush. "You are pretty when you're all cleaned up." He tucked me into his lap. "Someone is coming to look for a new pet today. Maybe they'll like you."

I curled up with my chin on his arm and closed my eyes. He stroked my back until I fell asleep. The sound of a truck rumbling outside startled me awake and my whole body began to shake.

"Don't worry," John said. "It's not that same truck."

A few minutes later, the door to John's office opened and a man stepped inside, followed by a lady and then Derrick!

"That's my dog!" he cried out. "From school! That's Little-D!"

I sat up in John's lap, so excited to see him again that I barked.

I am here!

The man held Derrick back so he couldn't get close. I could smell Derrick's fresh scent even from across the room— evergreens and sweetness. I wiggled in John's arms, but he held me tight. He didn't want the man to touch me.

The man scowled. "What happened to its leg?"

"He was trapped for dog-fighting bait," John said. "He's

lucky that truck crashed."

Derrick made a sad sound and tried to pull away from the man. "Little-D!"

The man's face darkened. He pointed to where The Spare used to be. "Why'd you take the leg?"

"Too much damage," John said. "But he's getting around well now. No infection. He's ready for a home."

The man stepped back and shook his head.

"Take the boy outside," he said sharply to the lady. His voice made me afraid.

Derrick reached for me. "No! He's mine!"

The man shoved Derrick's hands away. "No, he's not."

"Why not?"

"He's defective. We only want a beautiful dog. We're leaving."

He turned and pushed Derrick and the lady out the door. I cowered in John's arms, shaking violently until the sound of their truck faded away.

"I'm sorry about that, little one," John said, stroking my head and neck. "I guess you're a Lifer now."

I mourned the loss of Derrick for days. John kept me inside and set up a bed in his office. I had a special pen where he'd put me when I needed to be outside. There weren't as many dogs in this new pen, but we were all either old, or crippled, or otherwise undesirable. We were Lifers—without hope.

One day bled into the next. None of us Lifers ever left for

new homes. No one came to see us except a doctor who gave us pills and checked our old wounds. Whenever a new human came around, I cowered in the corner so they wouldn't see me. I didn't trust anyone except John.

At least not until a new doctor came from somewhere far, far away. I was out in the pen and saw her before she saw me. She was inside with John, looking over a sick dog. She had light eyes and smiled when she worked. Her hands moved softly over the patient and her voice lifted gently when she spoke. I sat by the window, watching her, longing for her to notice me.

When it looked like she was preparing to leave, I panicked. I needed her to see me! I howled and clawed at the window until John turned, the cigarette dangling from his lips. He smiled and pointed and said something to the lady. She turned to look, and all I could do was stand with my front paws perched on that windowsill, watching her watch me. My belly did this little tickle-flip thing.

John brought me inside to meet her. She felt calm and soothing, and when she took my chin between her fingers and tilted my face up to look into my eyes, I didn't resist. I did not feel afraid. I felt warm, like I was home. She examined the place where The Spare had been and cupped her hand gently over the old wound.

"What happened?"

"Truck crashed, crushed his leg. Had to come off."

"Did he have a family?"

"Not anymore. He's a Lifer."

She looked out to the yard, where a hundred dogs milled about, barking, scratching, sleeping, fighting. They were beautiful, strong dogs with four legs and no scars, all ready for a new family. She could have taken any one of them. I touched her hand with my nose so she would look back at me again. She stroked the top of my head and kissed me between the eyes.

"He's not a Lifer anymore, John. He wants to come home with me."

CHAPTER 8

I was in the back part of the clinic one afternoon, watching MomDoc finish getting an egg unstuck from a poor red chicken, when Toby came in. I knew right away he was upset. So did MomDoc.

"Hey, Tobes, what's up?" she asked.

"Mike sent me to pick up some medicine for one of the cats," he said.

MomDoc handed him a package. "You look a little rough around the edges. Everything okay?"

I came in for a good close-up whiff. Grass and dog poo—on both knees.

"It's just Huck." He swiped some dark hair away from his

forehead. "The dogs cringe when he walks by, and he called me slowpoke."

MomDoc held the chicken still and looked at Toby. "Slowpoke?"

"Yeah, he likes calling people names. Then he made me pull weeds in the play yard before it was cleaned up. I have to go home and change. I've got dog stuff all over my jeans."

"Where was Mike?"

"At the doctor, so Huck felt all big and important. Don't say anything, okay? My dad said I should ignore him, and I don't want him to think I can't handle the job. It's the only way I'll get my own dog."

"When I was thirteen, I might have punched Huck between the eyes," MomDoc said, holding her fist up, but then she smiled. "I won't say anything. Let me know if you need me to intercede. We'll get you that dog."

As if that wasn't enough for one afternoon, a lady with wild, matted hair came in to pick up her chicken after the egg was out, and made it clear she didn't like me. She pinned her eyes on me and snarled like she wanted to skin me alive.

"Why're you lettin' this dog run loose near my hen?"

Ozzie looked out from the office.

Whoa. Lady needs groomer.

"The hen is safe inside a cage," MomDoc said, bristling.

"It's a wild dog in them woods who did it to my chicken," the lady said. "Kilt one of 'em and scared the others so bad this one's egg got hung up."

"Where's the wild dog?"

"Up in the woods behind my place. Darn thing stalks 'em, but I shot it last time. Hit it, too, 'cuz it squealed and left a trail of blood. Dern no good dogs."

The lady took her chicken and squeezed it so tight on the way out that I thought the poor thing might never lay an egg again. As soon as she was gone, MomDoc came into the office and wrote something on a piece of paper.

"I'll call Mike later about the dog," she told me. "He can set a trap and we can get it some help. How much you want to bet it's not neutered?"

I was back out front later, hanging with a Boston terrier pup named Pugsly who was getting ready for the snip-snip, when a policeman rushed through the door carrying a gray-and-white, curly haired dog with a tiny tongue hanging out of her mouth. The policeman didn't even stop at the desk but went straight through to the back to find MomDoc.

Sorry, Pugs. I'll be back!

I ran after the policeman. He handed the dog over to MomDoc. "Found her in a car with the windows almost all the way up. Can you help her?"

Oh boy. I'd seen this before and it didn't always end well.

MomDoc laid the dog on a grate over the sink as gently as if she were a fragile egg and ran water over her body. Mom-Doc's tech, Smith, came up behind her.

"I need a temp, fast!" MomDoc said.

Ozzie jumped up and down behind the office gate.

Wuts happening? Wuts goin' on?

Heatstroke. Be quiet.

He sat down on his haunches.

Oh-my-dog, no.

Smith looked at the temperature-taking stick. "One-oh-five-point-eight!"

"IV fluids, now!" MomDoc said. She kept the water running over the dog. "Come on, sweetie. Cool down."

The policeman clenched his fists beside me. "Come on, little dog."

Smith stuck a needle in a front leg and attached a tube for the IV fluids. MomDoc put the little round silver thing against the dog's chest and listened.

"Heartbeat very fast." She lifted the dog's lips and looked inside. "Gums red and tacky. Increase fluid rate and let's get her some supplemental oxygen."

Smith put a mask over the dog's face and turned a knob on a machine that made a *whoosh-whoosh-whoosh* sound. Another machine made *beep-beep-beep-beep-beep* noises.

MomDoc and Smith worked quickly. Except for the beeping and the whooshing and the sound of water rushing over the dog's little body, everyone was quiet. Ozzie sat behind the office gate, watching. The policeman was beside me and the only noise he made was deep breaths. Even the receptionist didn't come back when new patients came in. We didn't see anyone until a girl burst through the door from the reception area.

"Hey!" The policeman stepped in front to block her. "You can't come in here!"

"They have my dog!"

She smelled of stress-sweat. Strands of pale hair stuck to her forehead and her eyes were wild and wet. Ozzie grabbed a squirrel from the pile in the office and tossed it over the gate.

Be happy!

I snapped at him.

Be still!

The girl tried to push her way in. "Squirt! I'm here! I'm sorry!"

MomDoc's head flew up and her eyes narrowed into slits. "If you want Squirt to live, you will stay back and be quiet!"

The girl sank against the wall and slapped her hands over her face. "Oh no, oh no."

A few more minutes went by. We were all still, watching MomDoc and Smith work to save Squirt. Finally, MomDoc turned off the water and put the silver circle against Squirt's chest again.

"Heartbeat is stabilizing a little."

She shined a light into Squirt's eyes, then moved the mask away and pushed her finger against her gums. "A little

74

better, keep this going."

The girl peeked from behind her hands. "Is she okay? Is she going to live?"

Squirt had been lying as still as a rag doll up until then, but when she heard the girl's voice, she moved her head ever so slightly. Everything was silent again for a few minutes. The policeman squeezed his fingers tight, then released them. Squeezed and released. The girl moved her hands away from her face and opened her eyes to look, cried once, then covered her face again.

"Smith, get her blood work," MomDoc said. "Stay with her. I'll be right back." Then she pointed at the girl. "You, come with me to the office."

Oooof!

Ozzie and I knew that tone. We scooted under the desk to get out of the way when they came in. MomDoc stood by the door with her arms crossed. Ozzie nudged me.

Girl in trouble.

"What were you thinking, leaving your dog in the car on a hot day like today?"

"I had to bring her with me. If my landlords find out I have a dog, I'll get kicked out. I'm in college. I can't afford another place."

"Why did you get a dog if you weren't allowed to have one?"

"I didn't plan on it, but Squirt was thrown out a car window and dumped on the side of a road! I saw the whole thing.

What would you have done?"

"How long ago was this?" the policeman asked.

"About three months."

"Did you report it?"

She shook her head. "I took her to my boyfriend's house, and we cleaned her up and wormed her and fed her and took care of her. I love her."

"And you've been leaving her in your car all summer?"

"No, no, never. I always dropped her off at my boyfriend's when I was going to class. My landlords say they're allergic to dogs, but Squirt is a Havanese, that hypoallergenic kind, so it's never bothered them. They don't even know she's there."

Ozzie looked at the girl and laid his chin on his paws.

Sad, sad girl.

"My boyfriend and I broke up so I can't take her there anymore. I'm going to do online classes so I can be at home until I figure something out, but I had to sign something for my professor. I was only inside for fifteen minutes, I swear."

"What is your name?" the policeman asked.

"Allison. Am I getting arrested?"

MomDoc and the policeman shared a look, then he said, "Not this time, thanks to Doc's quick work in saving your dog."

"She isn't saved yet," MomDoc said. She uncrossed her arms and went to sit near Allison. "I think she'll be okay but she's going to need to stay here for a few days."

Allison nodded and a new wave of tears rolled down her face.

Sad, sad girl.

"She's going to need a lot of IV fluids. Kidney failure is a secondary consequence of heatstroke. We won't know for twenty-four to forty-eight hours the outcome of that."

"But she'll be okay? How much will it cost? It doesn't matter, I'll find the money, I promise. Please save her."

Ozzie whined and MomDoc's face softened.

"I can't force you to relinquish Squirt this time. But if your landlords won't let you keep her, you need to do what is best and find her another home."

Allison clasped her hands to her chest. "I will, I promise. I love her so much. Can I see her now?"

"Just for a second. She's still recovering."

I followed along behind Allison when MomDoc took her to Squirt. She cried and leaned down close to her little dog's ear.

"I'm sorry. I love you so much. I will be back. Please get well."

The very tip of Squirt's wet tail tapped against the table. Her tiny pink tongue reached out and licked Allison's face. There wasn't anyone in that office who didn't know what that meant.

I love you, too. Forever.

After Allison left, the policeman laid some paper money on MomDoc's desk. "Put that toward her bill, would you?"

"That is incredibly kind. Much kinder than I'd be."

He shrugged. "I didn't look the other way when that dog needed me. I shouldn't look the other way when the girl does, either."

Squirt stayed at the clinic a few more days, until she was well enough to play outside with Ozzie. Then MomDoc let her go home. I was out front when Allison came, and I ran ahead to alert the others.

Squirt! Going home time!

Squirt and Ozzie bounced up and down together behind the office gate.

Home! Home!

Allison scooped up Squirt in her arms and kissed her all over. "You smell so good. I love you so much!"

MomDoc strode over. "Any news from your landlords?"

Allison hesitated just for a second, but then she smiled and said, "Yes! They said I can keep her!"

It felt to me like she was hiding a secret, but nobody asked her anything because we were watching Squirt wriggle in her arms and make those happy-whine-cooing noises that mean Extreme Joy.

"Just remember," MomDoc said. "We could have been handing you a box of ashes instead of a live dog today. Do the right thing by her."

Allison smushed Squirt's face against her cheeks. "Oh, I will, I will."

After they left, MomDoc sat down on the floor of the office with me and Ozzie cozied up beside her, each of us under an arm. She kissed the top of my head first, then Ozzie's.

"Somehow I don't think that's the last we're going to see of those two. I just hope it's under better circumstances next time."

I snuggled in beside her, grateful I didn't get left in hot cars and that I didn't have to live out on my own anymore, stealing chickens to stay alive.

HICKORY

The only thing standing between me and that fat speckled bird is a creek, a wall of old wire, and the threat of the human with the exploding stick. I don't see her outside the house today, but the leg where she shot me last time burns hot with fever. Something small and hard is still lodged in my thigh.

My stomach growls. That chicken will be tasty if I can get it without being seen.

I need food.

I slide quietly into the creek. The rush of water cools my wounded leg as I cross, so I hold my head up and push on to get swiftly to the other side. At the far bank I crouch in tall grass and wait, my eyes trained on the coop. Just one of those plump birds will feed me until my leg is healed and I can hunt deeper in the woods where it's safe—no humans with exploding sticks lurking among the trees and plenty of young rabbits just waiting to be dinner.

The wire fence has a weak spot at the bottom. The grass around that area is gone so the chickens can squeeze underneath and search for bugs outside the fringes of their yard. I can wait for one and be ready to pounce, or I can risk getting in and out faster than the human can hear them squawking and shoot me again.

My leg throbs after the strain of crossing the creek.

I lick my wound and wait.

The small human steps outside the house carrying a shiny bowl. He crosses the yard and his feet turn dark from dust. "Here, chick-chick-chick." He shakes the bowl and the birds run up and down the wire fence line.

Squawk!

Squawk!

He tosses handfuls of yellow corn into their yard. The chickens push and shove and peck the feed off the ground. The boy moves to the back side of the coop nearest where I hide and walks to the opening in the fence. He looks quickly back at the house, then throws more corn just outside of the pen so the birds will have to sneak under the wire to get to it. When the bowl is empty the boy looks almost right at me, then past the creek to the woods. He smiles and waves before turning away to leave.

The chickens peck and bob and fight for the chunkiest bits of corn. One bird, a small white one with skinny legs, has a bald spot on her head where the bossy birds make sure she knows she is at the bottom of the pecking order. She sees the corn the boy threw outside their pen. Slipping easily under the fence, she pecks fast before the others discover what she's found.

She is exactly what I waited for.

Her neck breaks swiftly in my jaw. There is barely a sound. No one sees me making off with her. No one shoots when I plunge into the creek. She is small enough. It isn't hard to carry her and swim to the other side. Maybe too small to feed me for long, but it was an easy kill. Once I am on solid ground, I hoist my injured limb up and move three-legged through the woods.

White feathers fall from my mouth and scatter among the dried leaves. At the collapsed shack where I hide, I crawl through the opening underneath piles of wooden beams and drag the chicken with me. The hole in my leg is packed with dirt again, but right now I can eat.

After the meat is gone, I sleep. When I awake it is dark and my leg burns. Fever racks my body. I lie on the earth floor and pant. By daylight, I am desperate for water. Not far from the shack is the trickle of a spring that feeds into the creek, but I am shackled by pain. I stretch out and wait for the throbbing to subside.

I am parched and dull in my mind and not sure how many days or nights have passed when the boy from the house pushes the standing door open and comes inside my shelter. His face is a fuzzy outline. He sees me in the corner and whispers human words I don't understand. He crawls beside me, pries my mouth open with his fingers, and dribbles drop- lets of water onto my tongue, then lays a cool, wet cloth over my wound. It is soothing and I am so weak I lie still and let him touch me.

Before he leaves, he puts a chunk of something brown and crusty he calls bread on the ground in front of my mouth. It smells sweet and I lick it with my tongue, then lift my head enough to bite a piece. Beneath the brown crust it is soft and fluffy. I gulp the whole thing and then let myself sleep.

It is dark when I wake, shivering. The boy has braced the door open with sticks, so I push myself up to get outside to the spring where I lap the water, then release hot dark pee onto a bush and stumble back in. My injured leg drags behind me, the toes leave marks in the soil. Pain pulses through my body. I throw up the water I just drank, then lie down on the dirt floor once more.

The boy comes again and brings a can of something fishy. He puts a silver bowl on the ground and taps the can until a lump of food falls out. I raise up enough to eat quickly before he can take it away. While I am eating, he holds the wet cloth against my thigh again and pushes until infection oozes out. With one big pop, pain shoots from the wound. I jerk my head around and yelp.

"It's okay," the boy says. He puts his hand on my shoulder and gently pushes me down. "This will make you well."

His tone is soothing. He is healing me. He rubs something sticky over the hole in my leg, then fills the bowl with water from the spring and leaves it next to another hunk of the crusty, sweet food.

"I know some other kid would call you Blue because of your eyes," he says. "But you look like a Hickory to me." He strokes the side of my face and props the door open again when he leaves.

Every night I shiver and pant in the dark, but every day the boy brings me something new. One day he tucks a soft blanket under my body. "So you don't have to lie in the dirt." That night, long after he is gone, I can still smell his scent on the blanket, and I am beginning to like it.

He brings me a hip joint from a cow, and I have that to chew on. He always has the crusty bread, sometimes a can of fish, sometimes a charred chicken leg, and he never forgets to leave fresh water. Day by day, the heat in my body eases and my leg doesn't burn as much. It is easier to get up to relieve myself, even with the leg dragging behind me, but I don't need to hunt for food. The boy will bring me something.

One morning, I am finally well enough to sit up and wait for him by the open door. My eyes are trained on the woods, watching for him. Something moves through the trees and my tail thumps on the ground, *thud-thud-thud*. The idea of him makes me happy.

But it isn't the boy.

It is three strange men carrying exploding sticks in their hands.

"Hey!" one of them yells, pointing at me. "There's a dog in there."

I back a few steps into the darkness of the shack and growl.

CHAPTER 9

We didn't go to the shelter very much at nighttime, but when Toby rode his bike over after dinner one evening and said there was an emergency, we made an exception. He came inside the house, his face dark, smelling like distress.

"Some hunters found that dog up in the woods, the one you called Mike about. We set a trap and got him this morning. He's at the shelter now, but he's hurt."

MomDoc looked alarmed. "Why didn't Mike call me?"

"He went home early. Huck promised he'd take care of it, but I kept waiting and waiting and he never called you. He just put the dog in the quarantine kennel and said it was mean. Then he locked everything up and made me leave. But that dog is hurting, so I came right here to get you."

MomDoc didn't hesitate. "Okay, I'll go take a look." She grabbed her keys from the shelf by the door. "Thanks for letting me know."

"Would it be okay if I came, too? I can call my dad and tell him."

"Sure, of course, if it's okay with him."

After Toby talked to his dad, we climbed into the car and I sat in his lap on the drive to the shelter.

"How long did it take to trap the dog?" MomDoc asked.

"We set it up yesterday morning and he was there today. He's got a bullet hole in his thigh."

"Ugh, I was hoping that chicken lady was exaggerating."

Toby wiped something from his eyes. "Why would someone do that to an animal?"

MomDoc didn't answer, she just turned in at the shelter and parked. When we got inside, we went down the hall to the quarantine room where a tricolor dog with blue eyes was panting in the back of the special kennel. I put my nose up to the gate and sniffed. Infection. And terror.

MomDoc will help you.

He licked his thigh where a wound was crusted with yellow pus.

"It sure looks like a bullet hole from here," MomDoc said.

The dog raised his lip and snapped. I jumped in front of the gate.

No! She's good.

He raised his lip again. The haunting smell of fear, and the way he cowered against the back wall, reminded me of the accident. The dog sank low and whimpered, his eyes wide and his ears pinned.

Help me!

"We need to tranquilize him before I can do anything," MomDoc said. She got the pole with the padded Y shape at the end.

"What should I do?" Toby asked.

"Well, you're going to have to help me a little here. I'm guessing you've never had to hold a dog down this way?"

Toby shook his head. "No, but I've seen videos. I can do it. I can help."

MomDoc glanced at him quickly and smiled. "You're an amazing kid, Toby. Nothing like the present to throw you into the water, I suppose."

He stepped forward and I got right up next to his feet. His hands were shaking a little, but he still said, "I'm okay. I want to do it."

"Okay, here's how it works. I'm going to go inside and put the Y part over his neck. It's padded, it won't hurt him. Then you come in and hold it really steady and firm. Don't let him up. I'll give him a sedative, then we both get out. Got it?"

Toby nodded, his eyes focused on the Y pole. "I've got it."

MomDoc opened the gate and went as far into the quarantine kennel as she needed to and swiftly lowered the Y onto the dog's neck, holding him still. Toby did everything perfectly. They were in and out quickly, and within a few minutes, the tricolored dog was knocked out.

MomDoc put her hand on Toby's back. "Good job, buddy. A rite of passage for a vet-of-the-future."

Toby's eyes crinkled at the corners. "Thanks." He pulled a piece of paper and some money from his pocket. "These were on top of the trap when we got him."

MomDoc read out loud. "*He was shot. I tried to help. I call him Hickory. Please help him. He's a good dog,*" she said. "Looks like it was written by a kid. At least he had someone who cared." She bent to look at Hickory again. "What would you guess, Toby, beagle-husky? Shepherd mix?"

Toby loved it when MomDoc asked his opinion. "Definitely beagle markings, but do beagles have blue eyes?"

"Depends on what they're mixed with. Nothing against Hickory, but he is a perfect example of why people need to neuter their dogs. He's been living alone in those woods, half feral and in all kinds of pain. Makes me sick."

They rolled Hickory onto a blanket, then moved him to the vet table out in the kennel room and switched on the overhead lights. Leroi came to her gate.

What's goin' on?

Wild dog, wounded leg.

Will it live?

MomDoc's on the case.

One by one all the dogs woke up. MomDoc and Toby worked on Hickory, and I made my way down the aisle. The little terrier with the torn ear was trying to push her head between the gate and the wall again.

Hey! Stop! You already hurt yourself doing that!

She jumped up and down.

Wanna see!

Moose was lying on his side by his gate.

Hey, big guy, how's it goin'? Any adoption prospects?

One. But my poo was too big. Mudder dint like that.

Just means it wasn't the right family. Don't worry.

I'd almost made my whole way around when I saw car lights pull up out front through the window. Mike's truck made a *rattle-rattle-shhhhh* sound. This made a *bruh-bruh-bruh* noise instead. Not Mike. Maybe someone leaving a dog in the drop pen? I trotted toward the office door, but Huck came barreling in before I got there, his eyes wild. MomDoc was filling a syringe with medicine when Huck saw Hickory laid out on the table.

"What's going on? Why are you here?" His eyes flitted

between the syringe and Hickory. "Oh, I see. You're gonna do it in, huh?"

MomDoc's head flew up. "Do what in? I'm giving him meds to help him get well." She put the needle into the back of Hickory's neck and pushed the plunger. "Toby was worried, so I said I'd come see if we could help him feel more comfortable overnight."

Huck peered at the leg from a distance and wrinkled his nose. "I just thought you'd get rid of it, with that leg and all. People don't usually want defective dogs."

Defective.

I knew what that meant.

I remembered.

A low growl rumbled in my throat.

"MahDi, stop," MomDoc said. "Huck, I'm not sure what your history with animals is, but here we try to help them, not destroy them."

Huck's face got tight and anger swirled around inside him, but as soon as MomDoc looked up, his expression changed and he smiled like he was embarrassed.

"Oh, of course, I didn't know. Sorry."

MomDoc worked the tweezer tool into the wound on Hickory's leg. She waved Toby closer. "Shine your flashlight down here for me, so I can see better."

I could smell the stench of infection from where I was, so

I knew she could smell it even without a super-sniffer. She didn't flinch. Because MomDoc lived to help animals.

"What made you pick a shelter for a temp job?" MomDoc asked Huck.

"'Cuz it was gonna be easy. My last job was really hard. I needed a break."

MomDoc looked up quickly and stared at Huck for a second with her mouth open. "I hope you're not disappointed by the amount of work involved."

Huck puffed his chest out and stuffed his thumbs in his belt loops. "Piece o' cake."

"Okay, good," MomDoc said. She went back to work and finally pulled a little clump of something dark out of Hickory's leg and held it up to the light.

"Looks like buckshot. Could be more in there, but this was what was causing the most trouble."

She dropped the piece of buckshot into a small container and cleaned the rest of the wound before placing a drain inside and closing the hole with some stitches. I followed Toby back to the quarantine kennel, where he laid Hickory gently on the cushion in the corner and stroked his head.

"Poor guy. I wish you could understand that we're safe."

Huck came in and hovered outside the kennel, looking down at Hickory on the bed.

"Dog's defective," he said to Toby with a snarky grin. "No

one'll want him. Shoulda been done with."

Toby bristled, but he didn't look away from Hickory. "He'll find a good home," he said.

"You think you know it all, don't you? How old are you, anyway?"

Lucky for Huck that MomDoc showed up right then so neither Toby nor I did what we wanted to do. MomDoc would be mad if I tried to bite, but I could have used his leg as a tree trunk and left it soaking wet. That was always the next best thing.

"Hey, how's he doing?" she asked.

"He's quiet, just starting to wake up. Can we wait with him?"

Huck stepped forward and puffed his chest out again. "I'll stay. It's my responsibility. You can go. It will be all right."

Toby looked up at MomDoc and everything about his expression was pleading for her not to make him leave right then. I went in and sat beside him.

MomDoc's eyes shifted to Huck for a second, then back to Toby.

"We can stay for a while and be sure Hickory's okay. Huck, you go on home. We'll let ourselves out and lock up."

Huck's dark little eyes squinted at me and he puckered his mouth. "It is late," he said. "I gotta be back early, so, okay, I guess."

After he left, Toby looked up at MomDoc. "'Okay, I guess'?"

MomDoc grinned and shrugged her shoulders. "Don't put one more second of thought into him. He's only here short term. Mike will be in and out of the hospital in a jiff and everything will go back to normal."

It was all the way dark outside when we dropped Toby off and got home, but the lights were on inside our house. Ozzie was standing on the back of the couch in the window, waiting for us. When he saw the car, he jumped down and was by the door when we walked in.

Who was hurt?

Wut happened?

Why didn't I get to go?

MomDoc picked him up and kissed his face. "You are so special, Oz, you know that?"

It was exactly what he needed. He snuggled into her arms, then tucked his head against the side of her neck and wagged that funny tail. A few minutes later we were all cozy on the couch, me on one side, Ozzie on the other, with Domino stretched out across the rolled back of the sofa behind us, purring loudly. MomDoc picked up the remote to turn on the television, but she just held it for a second, then put it back on the table and wrapped her arms around Ozzie and me.

Just before I drifted off to sleep I heard her whisper, "My little family."

CHAPTER 10

The next morning, MomDoc was muttering to herself on the drive to the clinic. She was worried about Hickory. I stood up on the console and leaned over to lick her cheek.

"MahDi, you can always read my mind," she said. "Okay, let's check on Hickory before work and see how he's doing."

She turned the car around and drove down the roads leading to the shelter instead of the clinic. I settled into the seat, feeling relieved by the new direction.

Toby's bike was on the porch when we got there. Ozzie saw it first.

Toby! Toby! Toby!

He was inside, sitting on the floor in Hickory's quarantine

kennel with his back against the wall and his hands resting in his lap. Hickory lay on the cushion in the corner. The infection still reeked, but he didn't snarl or look afraid because Toby was doing what Toby did best—getting a frightened dog to trust him.

"You're here early," MomDoc said.

"It was my first time to help Mike with a rescue. I thought about him all night."

"He seems calmer."

"He didn't want me in here at first, but he's better now. He'll get used to me, right, buddy?" He held his hand out. Hickory did not shy away.

"I'll give you some more time with him before I look at the leg. Where's Mike?"

"This is the day he went for his surgery," Toby said.

MomDoc squeezed the place between her eyes. It was the thing she did when she had forgotten about something. "Oh, darn, that's right. I meant to call him last night and say good luck. I'll check in with Rebecca later."

Toby put his hand on the floor between himself and Hickory. "He sniffed my arm a while ago. Gonna see if he'll do it again."

MomDoc and I left the two of them there. We knew if that scared, injured, part-feral dog was going to come around to anyone, it would be Toby.

Huck was back in the office. He was talking into the

speakerphone and writing a note on paper with one hand. The other hand was stuffed inside the giant bite-proof mitt Mike used in emergencies.

"Okay, I've got the address. I'll see what I can do. Good-bye."

He clicked the phone off and looked at MomDoc. "No one told me what to do in this case."

"What's up?" MomDoc asked.

For the first time, Huck smelled like he was wearing clean clothes, but there was still that lingering odor that I couldn't put my paw on. I tried to get close to sniff his boot, but he moved his foot when he saw me.

Loser.

"That was the hospital. A guy brought in last night keeps fretting about his dog, says it's at home alone. They want me to go get it, but I'm the only one here. I can't leave that kid here by himself, can I?"

I didn't like the way he called Toby "that kid," but I let it pass. Just this once.

"What did Mike tell you to do?"

"His wife is supposed to be here sometimes to help but not today. This is his surgery day. Do I just leave it there?"

MomDoc hesitated for a second, and I knew why. She was wondering how someone could think it was okay to leave a dog alone in a house for another whole day when it was probably scared and hungry.

"Where is the dog? Maybe I can get it and take it to the clinic with me, then bring it here later."

He handed her a piece of paper. "Not far, I think."

As soon as MomDoc's eyes hit the words on that paper, I knew. I *knew* something was very wrong. She put her hand to her mouth and her eyes got big.

"Oh no!"

"What?" Huck asked.

"This is my neighbor; the dog is Lilah!"

Lilah!

I ran in circles around MomDoc's legs, barking. Lilah was in trouble!

Huck plunked down into Rebecca's chair. "What's that mean?"

"Nothing. Don't worry about it. I'll go get her. I know where his spare key is. Come on, Di, let's go get your girl!"

Before we could leave, Toby came in from the quarantine room. His face was bright and his smile bigger than I'd ever seen.

"He let me pat him!"

"Who?" MomDoc asked.

"Hickory! He let me pat his front leg and he didn't growl or even raise his lip!"

"Oh no, I forgot about Hickory. I mean, that's great, Toby, but Mr. Crandle's gone to the hospital, and Lilah's been at the house all night alone. I have to go get her."

Toby brushed the hair from his forehead. "Do you want me to come with you?"

Huck sat up fast. "Hey, hey, no, I mean, why? You got work here to be done, remember?"

Toby looked from Huck to MomDoc.

"Stay here, Toby. Lilah will be fine with me. Rebecca won't be in today, so you stay and help Huck. I'll come after work and check in on Hickory."

I know for a fact that Toby did not want us walking out of the shelter right then, leaving him alone with Huck. But Lilah was in trouble, and there was nothing that would get in the way of our going to save her.

Lilah was watching out the front window when we got to Mr. Crandle's house. I could see her body start to wiggle when the car pulled up, and my insides started to quiver. Ozzie jumped from the far back of the car to the back seat, over and over, yipping and barking and wagging his tail. You'd have thought she was the love of his life, not mine.

It's Lilah! It's Lilah!

Mr. Crandle had a doggie door to the backyard, so she was okay in that department. But he didn't have an auto-waterer, so the first thing MomDoc did was fill Lilah's bowl and let her drink. She stroked her beautiful black fur while Lilah lapped the water.

"You poor thing, you must have been so afraid," she said.

Lilah sniffed my ear and face, then jumped to Ozzie to play, and the two of them ran all the way to the car, just like they'd been doing it every day of their lives. We were so late getting to the clinic that MomDoc didn't even stop and think about where to put Lilah, so I led her out front with me and showed her the bed she could lie on while I went to work. I loved letting her see how busy I was, and how important my job was every day. When there was a break, I'd go sit beside her and she would sniff me and bat her eyelashes, and every single time my heart would melt a little more.

What happened to your Mr. Crandle?

She lowered her head to the floor and looked up at me.

He was so sick. They came and got him and took him away. I didn't know what to do except wait.

I licked the spot between her eyes.

Don't worry. MomDoc will find out and you will come with us until he's home.

Thank you.

Then she closed her eyes and slept until Daisy came in near the end of the day with a red rash around her belly from the tutu. Daisy tugged away from her human-mom and trotted over to see Lilah.

What happened?

Her Mr. Crandle went to the hospital. She's staying with us for now.

Daisy always snorted a little when she sniffed, so when

she checked out Lilah's ear and face, the snorting noise woke my beauty up.

Hello, Daisy.

Hello, Lilah.

MomDoc called Daisy back soon, and when she left a while later, she had pink creamy medicine smeared in a circle around her middle and her human-mom was carrying a small bag of medicine. Daisy trotted out the door a lot easier than she'd come in when the rash was still hurting, and I knew that, Daisy being Daisy, every dog in our 'hood would know what had happened to Lilah long before we got home.

We went by the shelter again on the way home, just like Mom-Doc had promised. Toby was already gone, and Huck was in the kennel room, walking around with that big mitt still on his hand. Lilah was so excited to be with us, she and Ozzie ran through the aisle and bounced around playfully. Neither one of them was paying attention to Huck when Lilah accidentally bumped into his leg. She jolted to a stop and sat perfectly still, ears perked and her eyes focused on his face.

Huck curled his hands against his chest and backed up, his little dark eyes getting as big as I'd ever seen them.

"Ahhhhh! Get away!"

MomDoc grabbed Lilah's collar. "She's not going to hurt you, Huck. She was trained to stop and observe like that in case her owner fell."

Huck was backed all the way against the chain links of one of the kennels. He dropped his hands and scoffed. "I ain't afraid of her. She startled me, that's all."

MomDoc let go of Lilah's collar and waved her hand toward the back door. "Ozzie, Lilah, you all go outside to the play yard."

Ozzie and Lilah bounded away, but I stayed. Huck was all kinds of wound up. I didn't want him doing anything to MomDoc, but she shooed her hands at me and said it again.

"Go on out, it's okay."

I went as far as the door where I could still see MomDoc and Huck inside, plus Ozzie and Lilah outside. Ozzie grabbed toys out of the bin and started a game of tug-of-war with Lilah.

"I'm sorry about that, Huck, but honestly, Lilah wouldn't hurt a flea," MomDoc said.

Huck jammed the big mitt firmly onto his hand. "Nothing personal, but I'll be glad to get outta here and train for real police work."

"This *is* real police work. It's important work. A very nice policeman saved a dog's life the other day, found her in a hot car and brought her to the clinic. Do you think you'll be able to do that kind of thing when you're done training?"

Huck sucked his belly in and tried to look taller. "'Course. I didn't mean anything by it."

Then he waddled away, pulling up his big pants so they didn't fall down and expose his rear end.

Yes, it was tempting.

No, I didn't.

Stop laughing.

MomDoc went off to see about Hickory, but this time I didn't go kennel to kennel checking on the dogs like I usually would. I needed to keep Lilah out of Huck's sight. I nudged her and we went to the office with some toys and sat in front of the window by the door. We'd be ready to go as soon as MomDoc was done.

Sure enough, while we were waiting, Huck came into the room.

Lilah sniffed my face.

What's wrong?

I don't trust him.

Huck slammed a drawer shut and came out from around the desk.

"You must be the dog left behind," he said, eyeing Lilah in a way that made the hair on the back of my neck raise up. "Good thing someone was here to go rescue you, otherwise I mighta had to wait until tomorrow and you'd be peeing all over yourself by then."

He turned and walked out of the room.

❧ ❧ ❧

Lilah got to stay with us for three whole sleeps before we had to take her home. I gave her my beds and slept on the floor so I could protect her all night. As I'd suspected, Daisy had alerted everyone. Somehow, even Jimmy found out she was there and came down for a game of Rodeo with all the 'hood dogs. And when MomDoc and Ozzie hiked up the butte, Lilah played in the creek with me and we had a nap together in the sun.

That last day, when Mr. Crandle got back from the hospital, MomDoc and I walked Lilah home after work. We passed all the houses of our friends, but I couldn't even tell you if any of them were outside. I only had eyes for her. My heart sank a little more with each step, especially once I realized her attention was on the yellow house at the end of the road. Not on me.

Mr. Crandle was standing at the window, and as soon as he saw us he waved, and his face broke into a big smile. Lilah's tail swung hard side to side. She strained on the leash.

He's home! He's home!

Mr. Crandle opened the door wide. "Oh, my lovely girl, there you are."

Lilah could barely hold in her excitement. Mr. Crandle saw that I didn't want her to leave. He knew exactly how I felt. He touched the special heart bow tie at his neck.

"Thank you, MahDi, for taking such good care of my girl."

She walked away without even looking back and followed

him into the house. My heart sank to the bottom of my paws.

"Come on, Di," MomDoc said. "We'll see them again soon."

But I couldn't leave. I watched the window to see if she would come say goodbye, but there was nothing. Not even the tips of her ears danced by. That was it.

WILSON

My Boy is watching me through the window. Strange light makes his face look wet. He's not smiling. I am sad he's not smiling because when he smiles, everything is okay. Nothing feels okay right now.

The dad chained me to an old doghouse in the backyard. It is cold outside now, but it was hot today inside the house. This afternoon I panted because it was so hot and I drooled on the kitchen floor. The dad came home and slipped on my drool. He yelled things in the scary voice, first at me, then at my Boy.

It wasn't my Boy's fault. The dad said we weren't allowed to open the windows when he was gone. We were alone for a long time in the very hot house. So, I panted, then slobbered. On the floor. And now I have to stay outside because slobber is bad.

The dad pulls my Boy away from the window so I can't see him anymore. I creep backward into the crooked doghouse. I almost can't get all the way inside because the chain is too short, but if I hold my head a little sideways it doesn't pull so hard.

It's scary outside. There are so many new sounds. A *whoo-who-whooooo* and a *caw-caw* and some kind of dog howling that isn't a dog, really. It is something strange and wild that I'd never heard until we moved to this mountain. I shiver to warm myself and move a little closer to the wall so the chain isn't so tight on my neck.

Sometime in the night, when the sky is as black as my fur but the moon shines bright, I have to relieve myself. I move as far from the crooked, drafty doghouse as the chain will let me and make a puddle in the dirt. After I am back under the shelter, the dark yellow line trickles toward me. I don't want it to touch me, but I don't want to stay out in the cold and dark, either. I close my eyes so I won't see if the yellow line reaches me when I sleep.

In the morning, the dad's old truck cranks up and rumbles away. The earth in front of the doghouse is stained where the yellow liquid stopped a nose length away from me. I need to go again, but this time I pull the chain around to the other side and the yellow line trickles away.

After the dad has been gone awhile, the back door cracks open. My Boy pokes his head out, looks both ways, then steps onto the porch and closes the door gently so it doesn't make the banging sound. The dad hates the banging sound.

"Wilson!"

He tiptoes across the dirt yard and the bottoms of his superhero pajamas get coated with dust. He carries two bowls for me. My tail wags so hard I pull the chain and the whole doghouse jerks forward. It doesn't matter because my Boy has come back!

He places the bowls on the ground. I'm so happy to see him I wiggle and roll onto my back and tip half the water out. He laughs and watches me drink the rest, then I gulp my food so fast a bit gets stuck in my throat and I cough it all over him.

"Slow down! Not so fast, silly," he says.

He strokes the top of my head and my whole body feels warm and sunny. I wiggle some more and send the two bowls careening across the yard, so my Boy has to run after them. He picks them up and glances back at me, then looks toward the house, then at me again.

"Stay," he says. "I'll come right back."

I go to the front of the doghouse and sit to wait. Past the house, past the fields surrounding the house, dirt swirls up on the road and makes a cloud. It sounds like a truck. The dad drives a truck. Maybe it's the dad and maybe he'll untie me and let me go back inside.

I'll promise not to slobber ever again so the dad won't slip and fall.

I'll be really quiet when he is home and I won't lick his hand when he's watching the television.

I won't do anything he doesn't like.

Except breathe.

I think I do have to breathe.

The truck gets closer, but it sounds different. Lighter. Less rattled. Faster. When it passes the house, it isn't the dad's truck, it's a white car with two people inside who don't even know I am chained up all alone in the backyard.

I lay with my chin on my paws and watch the sun move until it is hovering straight above me in the sky. It is bright and hot again. How can this place be so hot when the sun is in the sky, and so cold when it changes to dark?

It is a long time before my Boy comes back, but when he does he is smiling. This time he is wearing pants that only go to his knees. He has his old sneakers on his feet, the ones where I chewed off the end.

"I'm back, Wilson!"

He says it in a light, happy way.

"Sorry I took so long, I had to wash my pajamas so Dad

doesn't see the dirt. He'd be mad."

My whole body wiggles and squirms and I can't help but make the noise that happens when I'm trying not to bark because the dad hates it when I bark. I roll onto my back for a scratch, but the chain gets tangled in my fur and pinches my skin. I yelp and scramble up.

"Hold on," my Boy says. He unclips the chain from my collar and steps back. "There you go. Let's play! Hurry, come on, before Dad gets home!"

He runs across to the other side of the yard. I burst away and chase him around and around until clouds of dirt rise from under our feet and coat his face and my eyes. He laughs and I run faster, but I never catch him.

It's the game we've always played, ever since I was a puppy and he was a teeny-tiny Boy. He runs, looking back and calling to me. I chase, but before I get too close I slow down, or pretend to trip and roll over and over until he is laughing so much stars shine in his eyes.

He pulls a ball out of his pocket and tosses it in the air. *Yay! Yay!*

I leap up and catch it in my mouth and drop it gently into his hands. He smiles even bigger and ruffles the fur on top of my head, then he does it again, and again, and again, and I am so happy I forget about being cold and alone last night. We are both so happy we don't think about how close we are to the house until my Boy throws the ball and I leap up to grab it, but instead of landing in my mouth, the ball bounces off my head and crashes through the glass window, making the most awful, horrible sound I've ever heard.

The only sound worse is the sob that comes from the Boy when he sees what I have done.

CHAPTER 11

'd been moping on the couch for days, missing Lilah. Mom-Doc had been busy working on a plan to organize a free snip-snip clinic. She'd had her head down and was tapping away at the buttons on her computer, not paying attention to anything else. Ozzie decided he was tired of being ignored. He came over to the couch and poked me with his nose.

Hey! Wanna play?

I put my chin on my paws and closed my eyes.

Okay, then.

He went off on his own. But a minute later, I saw him come around the front and onto the doorstep. He'd dug his way out of the backyard and was yip-yip-yipping, jumping off his hind legs like a bouncing tennis ball, his whole body covered in dirt.

Ha! Ha! I got out!

MomDoc rushed in from the kitchen and flung open the door. "You are so naughty!" she said, brushing clumps of soil and leaves from his wriggly body.

So much fun!

We both checked next door to see if Grumpy-Pants Lydia had heard him, but all was clear.

"Please, Ozzie, settle down and let me get this work done," MomDoc said. "We have lives to save."

Ozzie didn't understand *lives to save* and a few minutes later he had gone through the house, out his new escape route, and was back on the front step, yip-yip-yipping. Mom-Doc grabbed him and brought him in again.

"You rascal! How are you getting out?"

Ozzie peeled once around the living room, jumping from chair to coffee table to floor, and ending with his famous somersault off the end of the couch.

"Oh, crumb," MomDoc said. "Lydia's out in her yard. She's probably mad about all the noise." She shut the door quickly and turned to me. "MahDi, please explain how we ended up with a neighbor who hates dogs, and an escape-artist terrier with a wicked sense of humor?"

If I could talk, I would have reminded her that we'd saved Ozzie from The Unthinkable when we found him in an orange tag kennel with only one day to spare. That's how we ended up with an escape-artist terrier with a wicked sense of humor. The neighbor part I still didn't understand myself.

Ozzie stood at her feet, staring up with his bottom teeth stuck out and his tail wagging hard.

"Good grief, it's a good thing you're so adorable," she said, peeking out the window. "Okay, Lydia's gone. Let's go get ice cream. That'll be my very exciting midweek night. A date with my three boys."

As soon as they heard the words *ice* and *cream*, Ozzie ran to the door and Domino slunk around from the kitchen. MomDoc jangled the keys.

"If we want to escape without being detected, you're going to have to move a little faster, Domino. Ready? One, two, three, let's go!"

She swung the door open and the four of us bolted for the car. Me and Ozzie and Domino all jumped in and MomDoc eased the car down the driveway.

"Oh no, there she is," MomDoc said. "Just when we thought it was safe."

Sure enough, Lydia was running toward us from her house, waving both arms, her hair all bunched up tight around her head. Domino swatted Ozzie's rear end.

That's your fault, loudmouth.

"Let's just pretend," MomDoc said. She waved out the window. "Hi, Lydia! Gotta run!" Then she rolled that window up fast and pushed the gas pedal. "Ozzie, that's on you, buddy."

Ozzie studied MomDoc's face for a second, then put his front paws on the console between our seats and wagged his silly tail.

Yeah, but we get ice cream. . . .

Indeed. There was that.

Something crazy was happening at the shelter the next afternoon. Hickory was still in quarantine and Huck wasn't going to bring him to the clinic to be treated, so we'd been stopping in every day. This time, the white truck was parked out front. I started panting.

"Calm down, Di. I don't know what's going on, but it looks like they're bringing dogs into the shelter," MomDoc said.

She was right. The white-truck man handed a crate to Huck, who was still wearing that mitt on one hand, and Huck took it inside. Then Toby carried another one from the truck into the shelter. Then Huck came and got one more. Ozzie couldn't stand it. He jumped over MomDoc's shoulder to get out of the car and ran in looking for Rebecca.

"What's going on?" MomDoc asked.

The white-truck man wiped sweat from his forehead. "Fire over at Carsen County shelter. Had to get them animals out. Taking 'em all over this side of the state. Forty-five dogs and a bunch of cats."

"Forty-five, that's a lot of dogs!"

"Thanks for taking some," he said. "Everything's gonna be different now because all the shelters will be at capacity."

"What does that mean?" MomDoc asked.

The man shifted from one foot to the other. The smell of smoke spilled from the crates in the back. Smoke and fear.

"It means instead of me transporting dogs to other shelters to maybe get homes, I gotta take 'em to be euthanized. I hate that," he said.

He lifted out a small crate and passed it to MomDoc. Inside, a little black-and-brown spaniel with a strip of white down its nose was shaking so hard the crate swayed.

"How many are coming here?"

She set the crate on the ground and I went over to sniff. The spaniel put her nose to the gate.

Where am I?

Safe.

Promise?

Promise.

MomDoc and the truck man were still talking when Toby came back outside. This time there was a girl with a long ponytail following him. She had those freckle spots across her nose. Something about her was familiar, but I couldn't put my paw on exactly what.

"Doc, this is Beth," Toby said. The way his face flushed, I'm pretty sure he was blushing.

Beth shook MomDoc's hand. "Nice to meet you."

Toby pointed to the crate on the ground. "Why don't you get that little one and I'll get a bigger one."

The girl poked him with her elbow. "Why don't *you* get the little crate and I'll get the big one?" Then she stepped over to the truck and pointed inside. "Do they all come in?"

The truck man looked at her. "Huh?"

"All of them, are all of these dogs for us?"

"Oh yeah, they're all for here," he said.

The girl hopped up and pulled out the biggest crate, with a husky-mix inside. MomDoc, the man, and Toby all watched her heft the crate into her arms and carry it up the front porch steps.

"Anyone gonna open the door for a girl?" she asked.

MomDoc stared with her mouth open in a little *O* when Toby ran and swung the door wide for Beth. I didn't know where she had come from, but I liked her already.

Eight new dogs came to the shelter that day, all of them smelling of smoke and fear. In a shelter with only ten spaces plus the quarantine room, Huck and Toby had to double the new dogs up in empty kennels. Ozzie made trips back and forth from the Meet-'n'-Greet room, carrying toys and laying them in front of each gate. He dropped a stuffed duck with a bright colored beak by the spaniel.

Frens fur you!

Huck stacked the two smallest crates on top of each other in the aisle. I didn't like seeing that. Not one bit. It reminded me of all the wooden boxes tied together in the white truck before the accident. I had to be brave. I had to forget my past and help these scared dogs feel safe. It was my job. I trotted along the aisle, stopping to greet all the new dogs.

But besides the fire, and all the dogs coming, and the new girl, Beth, there was something else going on. Something about Mike. Huck went to the office to answer the phone, and when he came back his eyes looked like tiny black bullets. He huffed and puffed and marched down the aisle swinging his arms to MomDoc. She was crouched outside a kennel, watching one of the new dogs.

"So how do you like that?" Huck yelled.

MomDoc jumped up, and I circled around to stand between her and Huck.

"What's wrong?"

"Remember how Mike was only supposed to be gone a short time and then I could leave? Yeah, well, guess what? No such luck. He's gotta stay in the hospital longer!"

His cheeks puffed out, and if they'd been close to me, I would have loved to have taken a little piece right out of the center. I'm not a biting dog, really, I am not. But Huck made my hackles rise. He made my whole body itch.

"What happened to him?" MomDoc asked.

She was alarmed, but she was doing that thing where she kept her energy really quiet so everyone around her stayed calm. She had to do that all the time at the clinic when things got crazy.

"How should I know? Rebecca just said he'd taken a turn or something and he wouldn't be back right away, which also means she won't be coming until he's better. Which leaves just me and these two kids! Now what am I supposed to do?"

His voice had swung up into a high, sharp pitch that made me want to run away. But I didn't have to. He turned and stomped back down the aisle to the office. When he left, every being in that room, dog and human, let out a big breath and sighed.

In just the short time since Hickory had come to the shelter, Toby had gotten him to trust enough to let him put a leash on and go outside for breaks. He was still dragging the injured leg, but not as much, and the stench of infection was almost gone.

"You can tell he wasn't always wild," Toby said. "I mean, he had the kid who left the note doing something with him."

Beth must have been spending time with Hickory, too, because when we went to the quarantine kennel, she was sitting on the floor with one arm draped over Hickory's back. The other hand held an open book, and she was reading the words on the page out loud.

"Toby, where did Beth come from?" MomDoc asked quietly from the doorway.

Beth saw us. She closed the book and stood up. "I'll be right back, Hickory."

The tricolor dog looked over at me and stretched his front legs out comfortably.

Girl and Boy are good.

Beth came out of the kennel and leaned down to rub one hand over the top of my head.

"Hey, MahDi, I know who you are."

She had a nice, happy voice. Ozzie barreled around the corner from the office and catapulted himself into her.

"You must be Ozzie, you little rascal."

"Doc," Toby said. "Beth lives next door to you."

"Next door to me?"

Beth stood up and wiped her hands on her jeans. "My mom is Lydia."

MomDoc's eyes popped. "Lydia has a daughter?"

Beth nodded. "I was at my dad's until Mom got settled in the new house, so I just got here a few days ago. We wanted to come over to meet you yesterday, but I guess you were going somewhere."

Ozzie and I looked sheepishly at each other. That's why Lydia was running after us!

Ooops.

"Beth volunteered at the shelter in her old town," Toby said. He kept his eyes down and his face was getting flushed. "She came in to see if she could do it here, too, and then we found out we're neighbors. Rebecca said she could help me."

MomDoc looked from Toby to Beth, then down at me. "What a nice surprise!"

Beth was much tinier in size than Toby, but I could tell from the way he acted around her that she was mighty in heart.

"My mom said I can get a dog once we're settled," Beth said. She had no trouble looking MomDoc right in the eyes. "We had dogs at my old house."

"Really," MomDoc said. Not like it was a question, more like there was a mystery brewing.

"Yeah," Beth said. "Simple and Stretch. My dad's hunting dogs. They stayed with him after the divorce."

"Is that so?"

That's what was familiar about her. She smelled like Lydia, but also there was something else. Something soft and sweet. When she squatted down again to pat me and Ozzie, I got up close and took a big whiff near her neck.

She uses coconut shampoo, just like Lilah!

Huck stuck his head around the corner, his mouth all puckered like he was about to say something nasty. I was used to Toby getting tense when Huck came around, but when disgust wafted out of Beth, too, I jumped up. MomDoc flicked her fingers at me. Code for *Stop*.

"Hey, Huck, we're just checking on Hickory. I'll bring more antibiotics and give him a shot in the morning. Anything else

I can do for you while I'm here?"

He shook his head. "Nope, not till I know what the deal is with all those extra dogs. Supposed to get an email from the other shelter, but it ain't here yet."

Hickory looked up at Huck and raised his lip. He felt it, too. Toby and Beth might be okay, but Huck, not so much.

When we left for the clinic, Huck was sitting in Rebecca's chair with his feet on the desk, looking at his phone. Mom-Doc stopped before going out the door.

"If you need anything I can help with, you know where to find me," she said.

He didn't even look up. He just waved his hand that still had the giant no-bite mitt on it and laughed at something on his phone.

CHAPTER 12

O n Saturday evening, MomDoc went to see Rebecca at her home. It was pouring rain and the temperature had cooled down enough that she let me come with her, but I had to wait in the car.

"I'll be quick," she said.

I was a little miffed at being left behind and watched her run through the rain and into Mike and Rebecca's house.

Humpf.

She wasn't inside long, and when she came back she handed me a treat that smelled like Rebecca, then laid her forehead against the steering wheel for a second before we left.

"Well, MahDi, Mike's not going to be back for a little bit, so I promised Rebecca we'd keep an eye on the shelter."

If I could have spoken human, I would have said, *We're in this together.* But I couldn't, so I nudged her arm with my nose until she put her hand on my back and I could snuggle closer to her. We sat like that for another little bit until she turned the car on to go home.

"Since we're right close by, let's stop at the clinic and get Hickory's medicine for tomorrow. One less thing to do in the morning."

I made a little noise so she'd know I loved her, and she ruffled the hair around my neck, then kissed me between the eyes.

"You're the best Saturday night date a girl could ask for, you know that?"

The rain was beating hard on the windshield so she hunched over and gripped the steering wheel tight on the drive to the clinic. The wipers went *whoosh-whoosh-whoosh-whoosh*, flipping side to side, but they still weren't fast enough to keep the rain off. It was only a few steps from the car to the door, but it was enough for us to get soaked by the time we were on the covered porch. Then, the key jammed in the lock. MomDoc was wiggling it, trying to get it to open, when a car pulled up and flashed its lights.

"Who the—"

A man rolled down his window. Normally, this would put

me on full alert. It could even bring out a growl, it being nighttime and a strange person we didn't know. I held it back, though, because something told me this man needed help.

"Excuse me," he said. We could barely hear him over the sound of the rain drumming the roof of his car. "Are you the vet?"

"Yes, can I help you?"

"Please," the man said. He got out of the car and right away I knew there was a sick dog with him. "I've been driving around for hours because it's the only thing that helps Bailey."

He opened the back door. The car light switched on and inside, stretched out on the seat, was a handsome dog, his eyes closed and his beautiful, noble head resting on a pillow. Golden retriever with a little something else mixed in. He had soft pale hair with flecks of white around his eyes. Bailey tried to sit up and reach his nose for the man's hand.

"No, no, stay down, good boy," the man said. "Please, can I bring him in?"

MomDoc got the key unstuck and the door swung open.

"Yes, can you carry him in all right?"

The man nodded, then lifted Bailey in his arms and slogged through the puddles on the sidewalk. By the time he was inside the clinic, his shoes and the bottom of his jeans were soaked through, and his dark hair was dripping water into his eyes so you couldn't tell if it was rain or tears.

"Come this way," MomDoc said, turning on lights and leading him to the treatment area.

The man gently lowered Bailey onto the cushion MomDoc laid out for him on the exam table, then he stroked Bailey's face and head. The old dog didn't open his eyes.

"My name is Walter. I live closer to the other vet, so that's where I've always taken him," he said. "Bailey has cancer. They told me when we were ready they would help him go peacefully, but they're closed for the weekend. He ate a big breakfast this morning, we even went for a walk this afternoon, but then something changed starting about five o'clock. The only thing that has helped the pain has been driving him around in the car. I know he's at the end, I just can't make him wait until Monday. Can you help?"

MomDoc used the little round silver thing and listened all over Bailey's body. She examined his eyes and inside his mouth and pushed her finger against his gums. Bailey didn't make a sound, but when she was listening to his heart, he opened one eye and looked at me.

I'm leaving.

I stood on the stool next to the table, braced my paws on the edge, and got as close as I could.

I know.

MomDoc stroked Bailey's face. She knew exactly what Walter was feeling, and it always made her sad.

"You are doing the kindest thing for him," she said, looking at Walter's face. "His body is shutting down, but these dogs of ours are so loyal, he'll hold on through all the pain until he thinks you are okay. If you're ready, we'll move him into the Rainbow room. You can take all the time you need. I'm in no rush."

Walter cried when he lifted Bailey into his arms again. He carried him to the special rainbow-colored bed where the old dog would wait for his first welcoming sight of that Rainbow Bridge and laid him down gently. I followed to the doorway and peeked in. Bailey opened his eyes and searched for mine again.

Take care of my Walter. . . .

I lowered my head and tail.

Of course.

The last thing I saw before MomDoc shut the door was Walter sitting beside Bailey with his face buried in his fur.

"Come on, Di. They need privacy."

MomDoc and I huddled together on the floor of our office. She pulled me close in her arms.

"This one feels especially sad," she said. "That poor man, driving his dog around in the rain to try and keep him comfortable. Now I know why we had to come here tonight. It wasn't for the medicine after all, it was to be here for them."

I was out front in the clinic a few days later, hanging out with a leopard gecko named Roger who was in to see MomDoc about a wheezing problem, when Walter came in. His clothes still had Bailey's scent on them, but he also smelled like flowers. That's because he was holding a bunch of them behind his back.

Keep breathing, Roger, I gotta check this situation out.

I went up behind Walter at the reception desk and sniffed the flowers. Mums. If they were for MomDoc, he was going to be disappointed to find out she hated mums. Said they smelled like the bottom of an old shoe.

"I'm here to pick up my dog's ashes," Walter said to the receptionist.

Besides, Walter wasn't supposed to bring MomDoc flowers; that was opposite of regular. We took flowers to the people whose pets had gone over the Rainbow Bridge. This was most curious. I ran to the back to alert MomDoc, but when the receptionist said Walter was there, she brushed out her hair before she said to let him through.

Then, she brought him into our office. That wasn't regular, either. Ozzie peered at me from under the desk.

Sumtin' fishy goin' on here.

I know. I know.

I hadn't forgotten what Bailey had said. *Take care of my Walter.* So, I had to wait. I had to help if I could.

When MomDoc brought the wooden box with Bailey's ashes inside and gave it to Walter, I went and sat by his feet.

On the front of the box was a shiny gold plate with some words written on it. I can't read words, I only understand what some of them sound like. What was written on the gold plate didn't have a sound, but the way Walter touched it and smiled in this really sad way, I figured it was probably Bailey's name.

"This will hurt for a long time," he said.

MomDoc shifted in her chair. This was making her especially sad. I moved over and leaned against her leg.

"I understand how you feel," she said. "And I'm so sorry."

Walter kept looking at the box, running his hands over the top and the side. "Bailey was such a good dog. The best. He's been by my side his whole life. We hiked together, he went camping with me, he even has his very own life jacket for when we swim at the lake. Had, I mean. He had."

He tilted his head down and a little noise came from his throat when he said *had*. I went back to sit next to him and Ozzie took my place beside MomDoc. Sometimes just one dog can't dance fast enough to handle all the feels.

Walter rested his hand on my back. "I bet you're a really good dog, too."

"He is. He's going to save the world someday," MomDoc said. She touched the top of Ozzie's head. "Just like this one. The best."

"He's only got three legs. I don't know why I said that. It's not like you don't know."

"It's okay. It often surprises people, but MahDi is fine without. It was just a spare."

"MahDi is an interesting name."

"It means 'Good Dog,' which he is."

"Not Tripod," he said, smiling. "That's so cliché."

A new word. *Cliché.*

And it had to do with my name.

MomDoc had a thing called *a google* on her phone. When she needed to know something, she pushed a button, asked a question, and got an answer.

I didn't have a phone.

Or a google.

Or pockets to keep either one of them in.

"My daughter is the one who named Bailey," Walter said. "She gave him to me when she left for college. I raised her on my own and she knew I would miss her. Now I feel like there's a hole right here," he said, tapping his fingers against his chest.

If I'd been able to speak like a human, I would have told him what Bailey had said to me.

Take care of my Walter.

I knew exactly what he meant. But again, I can't speak like a human, so I had to wait for MomDoc to talk for me.

"What would you do if you lost MahDi or Ozzie?" he asked.

"You mean when? Because I will lose them someday and it will hurt. I'll cry a lot, then I'll do the only thing I know for sure that will make me smile again."

Walter scratched the top of my head thoughtfully. When he spoke again, his voice was soft, gentle, knowing.

"You'll find another dog who needs you."

I nudged his hand with my nose.

"Yes," MomDoc said. "Exactly."

CHAPTER 13

MomDoc held a clear glass bowl up to the light just outside the office door at the clinic.

"Lucy, you get an A plus for having the cleanest goldfish bowl in town!"

Tiny, pale-haired Lucy bounced on her toes and smiled. She always smelled sweet, like she'd been licking a candy-on-a-stick.

"Do you see how I put blue and green gravel on the bottom? That's so it shows off Mademoiselle's color. Don't you think she's remarkable? She has a double fantail and I'm teaching her French."

"Oh, I see, does she speak, too?"

"No, because she's underwater, but I'm pretty sure she understands. That plant in there is called *Anubias barteri*. It's African but it grows in Mademoiselle's bowl and she likes to hide in there."

"Such a vocabulary for a seven-year-old. Mademoiselle is certainly very lucky to have someone teach her so many interesting things. You are the epitome of fine pet owner-ship!"

Lucy nodded her head and her yellow pigtails bobbed. "I know what epitome means, and thank you. May I give MahDi and Ozzie their treats now?"

I didn't know what *epitome* meant, but Ozzie and I both knew there were certain people who came into the clinic who always had something for us. Lucy was one of them. As soon as she said the word *treats*, Ozzie jumped up and rushed to the gate.

I'ma ready!

MomDoc handed Lucy a paper mask, a yellow gown, and a pair of gloves. When she'd finished bundling herself up, her father gave her a pouch full of treats. Ozzie pushed me aside and shoved his head over the gate.

Oh boy! Oh boy! Oh boy!

Lucy always brought treats she made in her kitchen, not the kind that come in a box. Don't get me wrong, any treat is a good treat, but Lucy's were extra special. Peanut but-ter cookies this time. Maybe a little banana in there, too.

Yummy. One for me, one for Ozzie. Another for me, another for Ozzie.

"Thanks for making this possible," her dad said. "Her allergy is really minor, but her mother, you know, she's a worrier."

"That's why the first thing I'm going to do when I grow up is get a dog," Lucy said. "I'll start with a hypoallergenic breed, just to be safe."

"Which kind?" MomDoc asked.

"Mmmm, I think maybe a Havanese," Lucy said.

Ozzie perked up and did a little dance.

> *Habaneeze! Habaneeze! The dog from the hot car! She wuz a Habaneeze!*
>
> *Chill, Ozzie. Squirt has a human, remember?*
>
> *Ooof. That's right.*

"But maybe I'll get a poodle, or a bichon frise, or Maltese, or Shih Tzu. There are lots to choose from. Maybe I'll have one of each and I'll bake them special cookies every night."

She patted each of us on our heads, stripped off the gloves and gown and mask, and climbed onto the stool by the sink to wash her hands.

"I'm sure you know the reason Mademoiselle gets monthly vet checks isn't only for her, but also so Lucy can bring treats for the dogs," her father said.

MomDoc laughed. "I suspected, but no one here is complaining."

The father helped Lucy dry her hands, then lifted her to the floor.

"Thank you, a hundred bazillion times," Lucy said.

"If you ever get her mom to change her mind about a dog," MomDoc said, "I can find you something from the shelter. There was a hypoallergenic bichon frise not too long ago. Got snapped up pretty quickly, but just say the word."

"I'm afraid the only way any dog will ever come into our home is if it showed up on the front step in the middle of the night."

MomDoc winked. "I could make that happen."

Ozzie and I looked at each other at exactly the same time. MomDoc couldn't actually do that, could she? Humans had rules that dogs didn't, but neither of us really knew if this was one of them.

It was later in the afternoon when Toby and Beth came into the clinic leading a shaggy black dog with a broad nose and white tips on the end of his toes. No collar around his neck, but the kids had fashioned some sort of harness out of a bunch of leashes tied together.

The dog tried to sniff me but he had a stream of drool coming out the side of his mouth and I spun away. You'd have thought I'd tried to beat him with a stick, the way he hung his head.

Me bad dog?

Not bad, just the slobber. There's so much.

Bad dog has slobber. I sorry.

"Who is this?" MomDoc asked.

Beth rubbed her hand over the dog's head. "He was left outside the shelter last night. They didn't even put him in the drop pen, just tied him to the front door."

"Ugh," MomDoc said.

"Yeah," Toby said. "Look at his neck, he had a rope so tight around it's infected."

I got up close to MomDoc and looked when she pushed aside the fur around his neck. A string of drool fell from his mouth onto her arm.

Oh, gross.

I hate dog-slobber, but when MomDoc raised her hand to wipe it off, the black dog ducked. Like he thought she was going to hit him. When a dog's been hurt like that before, slobber doesn't matter. At least not as much. MomDoc rubbed the dog's head and he whined and panted and slobbered some more, but the whole time his tail was wagging so hard it could have taken down a fire hydrant.

"You poor thing, I'm not going to hurt you," MomDoc said. "Did Huck check for a microchip?"

Toby and Beth looked at each other. They understood the same thing I did about Huck. He wasn't like Mike.

Toby pushed his hand through his hair, his eyes brooding and dark. "I mean, he's Huck, and Huck is lazy. He wouldn't do anything with him, he just walks around with that mitt on his hand all day reading from the policy manual saying how we do everything wrong."

Toby's eyes flashed and Beth put a hand on his arm.

"We told Huck we were taking the dog for a walk, but we brought him here," she said.

"That's a long walk," MomDoc said.

"We didn't walk all the way," Toby said. "We walked to my house first and my dad drove us."

Beth's hand went to the black dog's head for a scratch. The dog looked at me hopefully.

Good humans?

The best.

I had good and not so good. Good is better.

"We named him Koda," Beth said. "Is that okay? It means 'friend.'"

"I think it's a perfect name," MomDoc said. She got soap and a wet cloth and gently cleaned around Koda's neck, then she smeared ointment on it. Ointment cures almost everything.

"He's not neutered yet," she said. "I'll keep him here overnight. We'll give him shots and the snip-snip tomorrow and send him back to the shelter."

Koda looked over at me with his eyebrows raised.

Snip-snip? Wassa snip-snip?

It means you go to sleep and wake up happier.

Oh. I wan snip-snip.

Trust me, MomDoc will be sure you get it.

Toby looked worried. "What do we say to Huck? We didn't tell him we were bringing him here."

MomDoc thought for a second. "Leave Huck to me. I'll call him. He'll be glad there's one less dog to worry about overnight."

Beth kneeled down and held Koda's face really close to hers. "You are a good dog. Even with your horrible breath you are a very, very good dog."

Thump. Thump. Thump.

Slobber. Slobber.

Thump. Thump.

That was his tail hitting the ground.

And him slobbering all over Beth's arm.

When we moved him to a crate in the back of the clinic, he didn't balk, he didn't fret, he didn't argue about going inside. He just climbed in, lapped up some water, circled twice, then burrowed into the blanket.

Nice 'n' dry in here.

Some dogs are grateful for anything you give them, even a steel crate in the back of a vet clinic. I trotted along behind MomDoc on the way to the car that evening, thinking of the people whose dogs had just gone over the Rainbow Bridge and trying to match this guy up to the home he deserved. He'd make a good companion for the right family. The best.

In the car, MomDoc put her hand on my back. "Don't worry, I know he deserves the very best home. And I think I might know just who that could be."

Oh, but for a human voice right then to ask the question. *Who?*

CHAPTER 14

omino was sitting by the front door, twitching his ears
back and forth, which is what he did instead of twitching his tail like other cats do. Because he didn't have a
tail, remember? Just a stub. So he twitched his ears instead.

Ozzie and I were in the living room, watching MomDoc
run up and down the stairs. First, she carried her suitcase
and set it by the door. Then Domino's crate, which is what
made his ears twitch. Then she stuffed a baggie of his food
into her backpack, plus his water dish, food bowl, and some
catnip.

"Catnip for a treat so you stay with me," she said, shaking a little container for Domino to see. "No escaping out

a window at Auntie's like last time. We have to be back by tomorrow evening and I can't go chasing you all over that town like before."

Twitch. Twitch.

Whatev.

After everything was loaded into the car, she tapped on her phone and put it to her ear. "Hey, Toby, Domino and I are leaving, you all set for tonight?"

Ozzie's head pivoted toward me.

Toby comin'? Heck-yeah, Toby!

No being naughty.

Me? Naughty? Wuts naughty wen I'm havin' fun?

MomDoc picked up Ozzie and kissed his face then put him on the sofa. "You be good, okay? Toby and Beth will be by to get you both in a few minutes. You're going to the shelter with them." She slipped us each a treat from her pocket and kissed my forehead. "Keep him in line, MahDi, okay? I love you."

MomDoc and Domino went to visit Auntie in another town far away every two months. Auntie lived in a big building where Ozzie and I couldn't go because it was full of old people, older even than Mr. Crandle. And more frail, too. Hard to imagine, I know, but humans are mysterious sometimes. Like cats.

Auntie loved Domino and so did all the other old, frail

people who lived in that same place with her. So, every other month, MomDoc packed a suitcase for herself and for Domino, and they drove away just to visit with her at dinner in the evening and at breakfast the next day. She said those visits fed Auntie's soul. I don't know if the soul-feeding part was for breakfast or dinner, I just know MomDoc never missed those trips.

"It's like how you make the shelter dogs feel more secure when you visit them, except I'm the only relative Auntie has left."

Toby and Beth rode up on their bikes a few minutes after MomDoc and Domino left. My paws started throbbing just thinking about having to run beside those bikes all the way to the shelter. Beth came inside first.

"We have a surprise for you guys! Come look!"

Ozzie ran out ahead of me and stopped short.

Huh? Wuts those things?

Toby's bike had a wicker basket strapped to the back, and Beth had a doggie-pack for me. I'd seen these before, mainly near the base of the butte when people carried their small dogs up to the top. But I'd never actually been in one myself.

I didn't think I'd like being strapped into something like that with no way to get out, but I have to admit, it was pretty comfy. Padded on the back, cushiony on the bottom, with a great view right over Beth's shoulder.

"You need to be rested when we get there, MahDi," Beth

said after she'd tucked me in. "Plenty of work for you today."

Toby put Ozzie into the wicker basket on the back of his bike and clipped two straps to his harness, one on each side.

"You're safe in here, Ozzie, and you can see everything!" he said.

Riding in the doggie-pack was the most fun trip to the shelter I could ever remember. Ozzie loved the way the wind blew his hair and ears away from his face, and he didn't try to jump out even once. But when we got to the shelter, Huck was sitting outside and the fun part was over. He had dark circles under his armpits again and stank like a swamp. Little beads of sweat dripped from his forehead.

"Look at you with that Dorothy basket hauling Toto all around town," he said. He took a puff off a cigarette and ground it out on the porch floor, then flicked the butt into the driveway. "Where's the defective one?"

A tiny growl rumbled in my throat.

"MahDi, stop," Beth said quietly. "That doesn't help."

Why do people always say that to me?

"Come on, Toby, let's go inside," Beth said.

They parked their bikes and off we went, but something was different. Meaning, more different than just Mike and Rebecca being gone. I sniffed around the bottom of the door to the kennel room. No sounds of barking or scratching at gates or anyone calling to me. Something was definitely wrong. Toby went down the hallway toward the quarantine room to see Hickory. Beth, Ozzie, and I went into the kennels. Every single gate was open. Every kennel was empty. All the dogs were gone.

Oh no! What if the white truck had been here to clear out some of the extra dogs?

Huck came up behind us looking frazzled and wiping sweat from his forehead with the giant no-bite mitt.

"Where is everyone?" Beth asked.

"Locked 'em outside," he said. "The noise, they wouldn't shut up, and that kid is the only one who can make 'em be quiet. It's getting on my nerves big-time."

"That kid as in Toby?"

One thing I'd learned about Beth was that she wasn't afraid to say whatever was on her mind. Not when it came to taking care of the animals, and not when it came to Toby. I loved Beth. I think Toby did, too. Our secret.

"Yeah," Huck sneered. "That kid as in Tooooobeeeeee."

Beth's face turned dark and fiery. Ozzie looked up at her, then at me.

Uh-oh. Trouble's comin'.

I'm pretty sure Beth would have decked Huck right there on the spot if Toby hadn't come in. And that would have been a very bad thing. That would have had *consequences*. That's the biggest word I know, and I learned it without a google or a phone or pockets.

"Where's Hickory?" Toby asked. "The quarantine kennel is empty."

Huck tapped the mitted hand with the other one. "Outside with the rest of 'em," he said. "I don't have time to walk him, and besides, he tries to bite."

"Outside? He can't go outside with other dogs yet!" Toby's voice was really high and stressed.

Huck puffed out his chest. "He can if I say he can. I'm in charge here, kid, not you."

"But Doc said he still has to stay separate until his leg is better!"

"Well, you ain't my boss and she ain't my mother. I make the rules around here until Mike gets back, and that's my rule. Shouldn't have a mean dog in here, anyway."

Beth took Toby's arm and pulled him away. "Let's get the leashes and bring them in," she said.

They went toward the back door to the play yard. Ozzie trotted along behind them, glancing back at me like he was bewildered by Huck's behavior. I wasn't. It was exactly what I'd come to expect from him. Stress, anger, tension, and excuses.

"If I'd known Mike was gonna get that sick and dump this place on me, I never woulda come here," he mumbled.

Beth spun around. "Mike didn't dump it on you, he's in the hospital. Do you even care that he's sick?"

She didn't wait for an answer, just followed Toby outside.

Huck looked down at me. "Yeah, what's your problem, Lame-O? Quit starin' at me. You're a creep."

A few seconds later, Toby was back carrying Hickory in his arms. Beth was behind him leading Koda, who was still wearing the cone-of-shame after the snip-snip. Ozzie ran alongside them.

> *No cone-o'-shame outside! You gotta tell 'im, Di! Koda might gets hurt!*

Leroi made a mad dash past them and bolted for her kennel.

> *Not supposed to be this way, MahDi.*

> *Everything's all wrong.*

A yellow dog with a giant head who'd come from the other shelter pushed through the door and shoved Beth and Koda to the ground. A tsunami of huskies and hounds and pit bulls and schnauzers jumped over the two of them, swarming the aisle, barking and yipping and howling, weaving in and out of the kennels like they couldn't find their way home. Ozzie was right in the middle of the pack, trying his best to direct traffic.

> *Hey, yellow dog, in here! Little spaniel, over here! No, wait, go back! Stop!*

Moose trotted in last, trampling Toby's feet, and lumbered to his kennel.

> *It ain't right, none o' this is right.*

Toby had flattened himself against the wall to let the dogs

pass, holding Hickory close up against his chest so his leg wouldn't get bumped. Huck ran from one end of the room to the other, waving his arms and yelling, "Shoo! Shoo!" until finally all the dogs except Hickory and Koda were back where they belonged. Huck slammed their gates shut.

"Why'd you do that?" he screamed.

"There wasn't any water out there for them!"

"And it's hot! They need to cool off and get hydrated," Beth said.

"Besides, they aren't all supposed to go out at the same time, there's too many of them," Toby said.

Huck's face puffed up and his eyes got really tiny and dark, like the piece of buckshot MomDoc had pulled out of Hickory's leg. He pounded his finger against his own chest.

"You're telling *me* there's too many of 'em? I know exactly how many is too many, it's all right there in the book, and I'm going to take care of it!"

He stomped his feet all the way out of the room and slammed the door. Beth wrapped her arms around Koda's middle. Toby was still holding Hickory in his arms, and Ozzie was sitting between them, panting. All the other dogs lapped water inside their kennels and crates.

"What did he mean by he's going to take care of it?" Beth asked.

"I don't know, but if he calls the guy in the white truck to take some away, they'll be euthanized."

"What do we do?"

Toby shook his head and looked around at all the dehy-drated dogs with their mouths in the water bowls. "I don't know. Something, but I don't know what yet."

After Hickory and Koda were taken back to their kennels, Beth and Toby went up and down the aisle refilling water bowls again, and I went to check on Leroi. She was lying on her bed with her front legs tucked and her ears back.

Where is Mike?

Her only link to Murph.

He'll be back.

I've never felt trapped here until today.

Trapped. I understood that better than she knew.

After the bike ride home, Beth and Toby sat outside on the deck eating ice cream.

"I don't know if I should call Doc and tell her, or wait till she gets back," Toby said.

Beth was letting Ozzie lick the last of the ice cream from her spoon. Ozzie was ignoring every rule MomDoc had about dogs ingesting dairy.

You'd better not get gassy tonight, Ozzie.

He finished off every speck until that spoon was shiny as a star.

I'll keep my butt to the window jussin case.

"I don't know, either," Beth said. "Except what could she do about it from far away?"

"I don't know, but everything is all messed up. I am one hundred percent positive Hickory wouldn't get his medicine if I didn't give it to him."

"Or get outside to pee, for that matter," Beth said. "Let's just see how things are tomorrow. Isn't Rebecca coming to help?"

Toby nodded. "Yeah, let's just get things calmed down while Huck isn't there. I bet he doesn't even know how to reach the transport guy, anyway."

Ozzie ran off around the side of the house and came back a few minutes later covered in dirt. Beth giggled and picked dried leaves off his face.

"Oh you silly, looking all fierce like you're wearing a superhero mask made of leaves."

Toby brushed away clumps of dirt, and for one second their hands touched. It was like an electric jolt zooming through the air. I knew exactly how that felt! Same way as when Lilah got close enough for me to smell her coconut shampoo and the peppermints. But Ozzie didn't feel it. He had a funny, concentrating look on his face. I knew exactly what that meant.

He was scheming.

CHAPTER 15

Ozzie stuck his wet nose inside my ear.

Wake up!

What's wrong? What happened?

Last I knew, Ozzie'd been asleep on the bed in the guest room snuggled up beside Toby. Now he was standing in front of my kitchen bed in the dark, his lower teeth shining from the deck lamp outside the glass door.

C'mon. We're goin' out.

Why?

Oh-my-dog, wadda-ya-mean, why? MomDoc's gone, it's time for fun!

It's the middle of the night.

I know it's middle of night, that's wut makes
it an adventure! Come on!

Maybe because it was dark and I'd been deep asleep, or maybe because MomDoc was gone and Toby was here but Domino was not and it had been a crazy kind of day at the shelter and I was still confused, or maybe it was just because Ozzie was so excited and happy, whatever it was, I let him convince me to go. He pushed through the doggie door from the laundry room to the garage and, after the plastic thing swung back, I went, too. The garage smelled like cut grass and Toby and gasoline, because that's where the mower-machine lived when Toby wasn't using it.

Ozzie disappeared underneath the worktable and pushed his way past some empty crates and three very large bags of birdseed. It was dark and musty back there, but not so dark that I couldn't see a mouse with a mouthful of sunflower seeds when it ran right underneath me.

Ozzie! Where are you?

Through the hole in the corner!

It wasn't just a hole, it was a dark tunnel. I didn't particularly like dark tunnels. But I went anyway because Ozzie was on the other side and somehow he thought this was going to be fun. I struggled to get all the way through because it's harder without The Spare, but when I came out to the other side, I was under the stars in the yard and Ozzie was so happy to see me he jumped around in circles.

Hot diggity-dog, you made it, Di!

That's your secret escape place?

Haha! Not telling—watch this new trick!

He pushed aside a loose board at the backyard fence, but this time he didn't wait for me. When I got through myself, he was already running off down the road in the dark. I didn't catch up to him until he was as far as Lilah's house.

Wanna go peek in Lilah's window? Maybe she'll come with us!

I looked longingly at the yellow house, but Lilah was too good. She was too dedicated to Mr. Crandle. She'd never leave him alone in the night to go on an Ozzie-adventure.

No, she needs to stay. Maybe we should go back, Oz.

No way! Let's go see the shelter-frens. I'll lead the way.

Ozzie didn't run off until he'd sniffed my face and knew I was okay. Out of breath, but okay. Then he trotted off ahead of me. We got to the path behind the two houses, and instead of going left toward the butte, he turned right on our short-cut to the shelter that we took when MomDoc wanted to walk instead of drive or ride her bike. It didn't matter that it was dark, either one of us could have found our way there alone. But by the time we got to the field at Toby's school, I was getting a little more worried.

I don't think we should be doing this!

Ozzie waited for me in the middle of the field.

Why not?

What if Toby wakes up?

Oh-my-dog, Di, it's an adventure! Jus c'mon.

I limped along behind him, mainly because I didn't think he should go on alone. There was a big road we'd have to cross up ahead and we didn't have MomDoc with us to stop cars from coming like she always did before. It was just me and Ozzie and a dark night. I barked a warning.

Be careful!

When I came up the hill from the woods to the road, he'd already made his way across and was waiting on the other side, watching for me in the yellow glow of the streetlamps. My pads were sore from running so fast on pavement, my back leg throbbed, and I was out of breath. Adventure or no, I needed a break, but Ozzie got impatient.

C'mon!

Gimme a second here.

One of my front paws was bleeding. Just a drop. I licked it clean, then moved to the edge of the road to cross. Tires squealed and a car sped up the hill. Bright lights blinded me. It was one of those cars that didn't have a top on it, so I could hear the boys inside laughing and the music blaring and the engine roaring. I froze, watching it barrel toward me. The last thing I heard was one of the boys yelling, "Hey, look out for that dog!"

Then a *bam!* and everything went dark.

QUINN

The clapping stopped hours ago, but my heart pounds hard in my chest as it always does after an agility trial. I am still a champion, even though I limped off the course today. Marilease says so. Things are about to change. I know that because she knew I was hurting again.

"Here's your Stuffy," she says, handing me my personal toy companion I've had ever since I can remember. I tuck Stuffy in the space beside me and the wall of my crate and lie down. "You are always my champion, Quinn. No matter what."

And when she said *no matter what*, I knew I'd let her down. No matter how hard I tried, no matter how many hands clapped and yelled for me when I was on an agility course, no matter how obedient I was and how swiftly I followed her signals, none of that mattered because I'd let the judges see my hips hurt. I was done for.

After we get home, Marilease brings me and Stuffy to the living room so she and Justin can cook dinner and talk. I hear everything.

"She can be a house dog, Justin, she doesn't have to compete," Marilease says.

The smells of tomato sauce and spices drift from the kitchen to my spot where I rest on my living room bed. No amount of licking makes my hips stop hurting, so I lick the spot on Stuffy's face where Marilease had to sew him back up after another dog tried to take him from me.

"I've always promised her to my mom," Justin says. "She loves—"

"Your mom is too fragile to care for a parakeet. What makes you think she'll be able to walk Quinn every day?"

Marilease comes into the living room with my medicine wrapped inside a soft, squishy treat. "Here you are, sweet girl."

I take it from her fingers and roll onto my side so she can scratch my belly before going back to duke it out with Justin. I can see the mantel over the fireplace stacked with shiny trophies we've won together. Marilease rubs her fingers between my eyes and smiles.

"Your sweet white spot, Quinn, it's the angel who will always watch over you."

The soft warmth of medicine washes over me. I close my eyes and drift away to the sound of dishes clanking and Marilease and Justin arguing over what to do with me.

Justin wins. On their next trip to agility trials we stop overnight at Justin's mother's house. My last glimpse inside the back of the van where I've traveled with them for years is when Marilease brings me with her to fill water bowls before they head off. She is crying and talks to me while she works.

"Lois is super nice, Quinn, she's just old. But maybe you'll like being quiet for a while, not having to go on the road and hear all the noise and feel all the commotion. I mean, what kind of life have you had, cooped up all the time when we travel, then brought out for people to watch you work? You're a heeler, a cattle dog, you were bred to work, but sheesh, maybe it will be nice to rest a little, don't you think?"

She sniffles and wipes under her nose with the back of her hand and doesn't hear me when I whine. I am not supposed to whine or bark. Ever. No matter what. But her sadness weighs on me, sinks me low, and I can't help it.

"There is a kid who is going to come take you out every day to play. If you don't want to play, just lie down."

When she says these words, I lie on the concrete sidewalk by her feet, waiting for her next command. She sees me and her face wrinkles and she squats and rubs both hands all up and down my body, and I think for a second she isn't going to leave me there, she's going to let me come no matter what Justin says. But she doesn't. She wipes her eyes with the bottom of her T-shirt, closes the doors to the van, and yells out loud.

"Justin!"

Then she hoists me and Stuffy into her arms and carries me to the house and sets me down in front of my new person, Lois, who has white hair and uses a stick to walk.

Stuffy still smells like Marilease, and I believe this means she will be back. Every day, we watch through the slim window beside the front door, waiting for her. Without the dependable rhythm of competing, I don't know when one day is different from the day before. I sleep so much, almost as much as Lois, and I get confused.

Sometimes Lois forgets to feed me. Other times she forgets that she already has and gives me two or three breakfasts. When I refuse food, she calls Justin on the phone and he tells her not to worry. This is what she says to me.

"Justin says not to worry, that you know how much to eat and when, so . . ." She leans over, bracing herself on her cane and scratches between my ears. "I hope you're happy here, Quinn. I don't know how to tell."

The girl called Sarah comes every day to take me for a walk. She is friendly and pats me and takes a lot of pictures on her phone.

"You have this little white spot between your eyes that looks like a snow angel. Almost perfect." She snaps another picture and says she is sending it to her friends.

Sarah doesn't understand that walking on the pavement hurts my hips, especially on days that Lois forgets my medicine. When I pull on my leash so Sarah will move over to walk on the grass, she laughs and thinks it has something to do with agility, so she takes more pictures and we keep walking down the middle of the sidewalk.

One day Lois doesn't get out of bed in the morning to let me out in the backyard. It is a long time before Sarah comes, and as soon as she opens the front door, I race past her and relieve myself under the bushes. Sarah laughs and takes another picture.

Lois doesn't answer when Sarah calls upstairs. She shrugs and says, "Maybe she's taking a nap." Then she clips the leash on my collar and we go for our walk. This happens the next day, too, but the third day, Sarah's father comes with her. Then other people come and they carry Lois out on a bed and she mumbles something about Justin.

I've had no food for three days other than the treats Sarah gives me and what I could get from tipping over the trash can, but I perk up when I hear Justin's name. Sarah's father and another man talk while Sarah sits on the couch and cries. I lie at her feet holding Stuffy tight in my mouth, hoping she'll make them say Justin's name again.

"Oh, Quinn, if I had only known, I would have thought to check on Lois. I feel awful!"

A new rush of tears floods down her face. She leans forward to cradle me in her arms, but still no one says Justin's name again.

"We'll get ahold of someone to come get you, Quinn, don't worry," Sarah's father says. He has kind eyes and I am sure he means it.

They fill my water bowl and leave blankets on the floor and the kitchen light on. Then they close the front door and, except for Stuffy, I am alone.

I dream of hands clapping and whistles blowing and flags flapping and crate doors snapping shut, and I smell the excitement coming from the crowd. I see Marilease's pale hand signaling my next obstacle, and I feel the air underneath me as I fly over each fence, or race through each tunnel.

When I startle awake, I jump up ready to compete. My heart is racing and I'm excited and happy and look in the dark for Marilease, and then I remember she isn't here. I am not there. They went without me. I need to relieve myself, but at Lois's house there is no dog door to get outside on my own. I have to wait for someone to return the next day.

I lower myself slowly to my bed, wincing when my hips hit the cushion because no one thought to give me my pain medicine. Again.

CHAPTER 16

When I awoke, the lights were bright and hurt my eyes. Someone hovered over me. A boy who wasn't Toby shined a flashlight in my face.

"I think he's okay!" he called out. "He's breathing."

My whole body was shaking and my head was woozy. Nothing hurt yet and the thing I smelled most wasn't blood like in the white-truck accident so long ago—it was burning rubber. I sat up on the gravel and shook my head. Ozzie sniffed me from behind.

You k, Di? You gonna be k?

He licked my ear and put his chin over my back. In the dark I could just make out a few other people standing next to the car with no top. Now it was missing a tire, too. Chunks of rubber were scattered across the road. I was woozy in the head and didn't move when the boy kneeled beside me and touched my back. He smelled of sweet smoke. Another boy walked slowly over, puffing on a cigarette.

"Can he walk?"

The sweet-smoky boy put his hands under my belly and lifted me up, but as soon as he saw I didn't have The Spare, he screamed and let go.

"Did we do that?"

Ozzie jumped between us and faced them, his little body tiny but mighty. He didn't growl, but the boys knew he meant business.

"Okay, little warrior, okay, we won't touch him."

Cigarette-boy looked at my back end.

"We didn't do that, he's a tripod. I bet he just startled and fell down when the tire blew. We were right beside him."

Sweet-smoky boy stuffed his hands in his jacket pockets and looked around in the dark. "What are they doing out here in the middle of the night? Maybe we should take them with us."

I wasn't steady on my paws yet, and the whole episode was starting to sink in and frighten me, but I understood perfectly what that boy meant. No way were we going anywhere except to our own home. Ozzie snuck up close and made a small noise.

Run?

I took one small step to see just how wobbly my legs were, then barked.

Now! Let's go!

I launched myself away and tumbled down the hill into the woods. Ozzie ran beside me the whole way. The two of us bolted through the trees and raced toward the path that would take us back to our 'hood and then home. We were long gone before the boys even found their way to the bottom of the hill. At the fence by our backyard, Ozzie held the loose board aside with his head for me to go through first.

Sorry, Di . . .

I knew he was sorry, but I was only interested in getting inside. The whole day and night were too much for me. My pads hurt from scrambling over twigs and thorny branches in the woods and then running on the pavement. One whole side of my body was already feeling battered and bruised, and I couldn't stop thinking about how close I'd come to another terrible accident. I crawled onto my kitchen bed and closed my eyes. Ozzie curled up beside me.

You k, Di?

Go to sleep.

That wasn't much fun, Di.

No, not much fun at all.

The next morning I limped to the door for Toby to let us out-side. Every inch of my body throbbed and ached.

"What's wrong, Di?" Toby asked. "You're limping."

He watched me go under the bushes to do my business, then lifted me gently and carried me to the couch. "Doc and Domino will be home soon."

Ozzie stood beside the sofa and peered at me, his little eyes so sad.

Sorry you got hurt, Di.

Me, too.

Toby left us at home when he and Beth went to the shel-ter, so we didn't get to see Rebecca, but I didn't want to go, anyway. I wanted to sleep and make the memory of the *bam!* sound of the tire blowing up beside me go away. It was nearly dinnertime when MomDoc and Domino got back. Toby was sitting on the sofa with us, watching television, but as soon as he heard the car outside, he got out his phone and called Beth. A few minutes later, after the welcome-home chaos that happens at the front door when MomDoc has been away over-night, Beth and Toby were at the kitchen table telling her all about Huck making the dogs stay outside without water.

"And he said he was going to take care of the overcrowding problem. What do you think he means by that?" Toby asked.

MomDoc rubbed her fingers across her forehead. She was more weary than usual after she'd been to see Auntie.

I pushed her hand with my nose and made a little *I love you* sound.

"I don't know what he thinks he can do other than working harder to get those dogs adopted out," she said. "How many are still there from the fire rescue?"

Toby and Beth looked at each other and counted. "Five of the eight, so with the others already there we still have two kennels doubled up."

"We're a small shelter, but still, that's not really horrible. Unless you're Huck, I guess. I'll calm him down in the morning, and we can also work on finding temporary fosters until Mike gets back."

Beth and Toby looked at each other again and Beth nodded silently. "You tell her."

"There's more, though," Toby said. "We don't think he's feeding the animals on the regular schedule, and he won't put anyone outside until we get there."

"Yeah," Beth said, "and he won't clean the kennels."

"Why won't he clean them?"

"Bunions," Toby said.

Bunions. That sounded like onions and those made Mom-Doc cry.

Beth waved her hand in front of her face the same way Mrs. Peabody always did about Peabody's problem. "He took his boots off to prove it. Smelled like the bottom of a wet horse stall."

MomDoc didn't say much else about Huck, she just looked beaten down. Tired. Worried. But not just about the shelter, there was something else on her mind. Domino told us after she had gone to bed.

Auntie's sick.

He didn't know what kind of sick. All he knew was that Auntie was going to have to live somewhere else besides in the building with the other old people. And Domino was extra agitated by the whole visit because they wouldn't let him sit in Auntie's lap.

They said it wasn't safe. That made her cry.

He climbed onto the back of the sofa and sat very still. You would have thought he was a toy cat in a store window if it hadn't been for his ears twitching.

I don't like that.

He stretched out and stared at the night. Ozzie put his paws up on the sofa.

She comin' to live here?

Domino didn't answer, he just closed his eye and ignored him. Ozzie didn't like being ignored, and besides, he was worried. He jumped onto the seat and nudged Domino.

You hear me? She comin' here?

Domino's ears twitched again. He yawned really big, like he might be getting ready for a nap, then —

Swat!

One white-tipped paw flew across Ozzie's face. He flipped

backward off the sofa, landed on his side, rolled into a ball, jumped up, yipped and howled and ran upstairs to MomDoc. Domino focused his one eye on me.

Think he'll ever learn?

MomDoc told Huck the next day that she'd work on finding fosters to take some of the dogs until Mike got back. His eyes flashed when she said that he couldn't call the white-truck guy to come pick up any dogs, but he didn't say anything about it. He just walked away.

I was still a little sore a couple of days later when we made a vet visit to a ranch near the base of the big mountains. We didn't do much ranch work anymore, but early in the morning MomDoc got a call from a lady who raised sheep. She had an injured lamb and couldn't bring it to town, so we drove out to her before going to the clinic. Ozzie was miffed he had to stay behind.

Oof! Why not? Ranches r heck o' fun!

He would have been disappointed. It wasn't a nice ranch visit. The lamb was past saving and the mother sheep was running around the pasture bleating for her baby while the others in her flock stood by and watched. We met the ranch lady about halfway up her long, rocky driveway, next to a pasture bordered by rough wooden fences. A large white dog with a curly tail watched from nearby, his head hanging down. He was embarrassed about something.

The ranch lady flung her hand and stamped her foot, and a poof of dust rose around her. "Useless! Get!"

The poor dog slunk away. He turned back once to see if maybe she'd changed her mind, but no such luck. She clenched her fists and snarled.

"Git, I said!"

He lay down underneath a pickup truck and tucked his face between his paws. MomDoc scowled.

"Poor thing, he looks so sad."

The ranch lady didn't like her saying that. She thrust her hands onto her hips and scowled. "He should be sad. He's responsible for this. If he was a better guard dog—never mind. The lamb is a goner. That's all that matters. Let's get this over with."

MomDoc took out a syringe and a tube of the medicine that sends animals over the Rainbow Bridge, and kneeled beside the lamb. I went to the dog.

What happened?

He blinked both eyes really fast—a sign of shame.

I'm useless.

Not useless.

I wanna go with the kids to swim. I don' wanna watch sheep.

You just have the wrong job.

The mother sheep was running along the fence, bleating, but her little white lamb was already gone. The rest of the flock huddled together to watch, and when the mother finally stopped crying, they all dropped their heads and ripped grass from the earth.

"I can't send them up on the mountain without a dog, and this pasture will be grazed down too soon," the ranch lady said. "I paid a lot of money for that dog, but he's useless as a guardian."

The dog turned his head away and covered his ear with a large white paw.

"Listen," MomDoc said. "The shelter is full right now and there are a couple of big mountain dogs. Maybe one of them will work?"

The lady shook her head. "I have to have trained guardian breeds, not big lugs who lie around and eat too much."

"I understand," MomDoc said. "Just please don't take this one to the shelter, he'd just get sent off to be euthanized."

The ranch lady shrugged like *so what*.

"If you decide not to keep him, call me directly. You've got my number. I'll find him a home myself."

The lady didn't answer, she just turned and walked away, her shoulders drooping and her jeans covered in the dust of a hard ranch life. When she got near the truck, the dog scrambled out from underneath and ran away from her.

"We named you Hero for a reason," she said to him. "But you're useless."

We drove down the long driveway and I looked out the back window. Hero was sitting near the dead lamb. He wasn't interested in it; he was watching us leave like he wished he could come with us. Like he'd much rather be anywhere else on earth besides where he was right then.

You probably think dogs can't feel things like gratitude, but I'm telling you we can. And we do. I nuzzled MomDoc's arm, and when she lifted it up, I tucked myself underneath for the rest of the ride to the clinic. I know we were thinking the same thing—who would be the perfect family for a hairy, one-hundred-pound dog who'd failed as a guardian of sheep but would give his own life to protect children?

The clinic waiting room was packed when we got there. I went right to work, checking in first with Fred the boxer, who was back again, sitting beside his dad. One of his paws was wrapped in white gauze and a spot of blood seeped from the side.

Porcupine?

Glass.

Sorry, buddy.

I made my way around the room, but I couldn't stop think-ing about all the dogs still at the shelter waiting for new homes. Whenever someone came into the clinic without a dog in tow, I went right over and scouted around, checking to see if I detected the scent of one at home. A person without a dog already might be ready to add to their family.

The only person who didn't smell like dog was a short man with no hair on his head. He smelled of cats. Like maybe there were a dozen of them crawling all over his house. When he saw me coming, he turned his shoulder and puckered his mouth all tight.

"Go away."

He would definitely not do. I went to the office to wait for lunch. Ozzie was still at home with Domino, which meant I'd get all the attention, plus the extra goodies MomDoc had packed. I'd smelled tuna all the way to the ranch, then all the way back, so I knew there was that. I just wasn't sure what else might be in her bag. Maybe something gooey or stinky just for me.

Plus, she'd be able to tell me over and over how brilliant I was while dropping those treats into my mouth because she wouldn't have to worry about hurting Ozzie's feelings. I closed my eyes to think about what she might say, but my lovely moment was interrupted when Walter poked his head around the corner.

"Anyone hungry?"

He waved a paper bag around that smelled of beef and grease and sweetbread and pickles. MomDoc looked up from a cat she'd been treating for an ear infection. Her face got all shiny and happy.

Yuck.

"Ooo, my favorite sandwich place! Come on back!"

Whatever.

This wasn't the first time Walter had shown up since Bailey had gone over the Rainbow Bridge. After he came for the ashes and gave MomDoc the flowers, he dropped off a card and waited to tell her in person that he'd forgotten to give it to her before. Like we believed that. Then he brought a plant that was still sitting on the windowsill of our office.

Our office!

A few days later, MomDoc had put on fancy clothes and left me and Ozzie and Domino at home while she and Walter went out together.

They stayed out long after dark.

When they came back, her face was flushed.

I didn't like it one bit.

Bailey had said for me to take care of his Walter, but he meant for me to find him another companion—not let him make MomDoc all swoony. I fretted the whole time they were gone that night. Domino lay on the back of the sofa watching me. He couldn't care less about Walter hanging around so long as he got his dinner on time and a spot on top of Mom-Doc's feet in bed at night.

One night, Ozzie and I had heard Walter's car pull up at

the same time and crashed into each other trying to be the first to the door. Domino sauntered past, twitching his ears and watching me with his one eye.

Sucker. Someday you'll learn how to work the humans.

But that day, when I should have had MomDoc all to myself at the clinic, she didn't come to the office for lunch like she usually did. She and Walter set their sandwiches out in the treatment room like they were having a picnic. I lay under the desk, moping, and trying not to hear them laugh together. Before he left, Walter came in and leaned down to peer at me.

"You didn't think I'd forget, did you, MahDi?"

He held out a small bag of super-smelly liver treats. Did MomDoc know he was giving me liver? Or was he trying to get me into trouble? I turned my head and ignored him.

"Playing hard to get? Here, let me help you out of that."

He dropped a handful of lusciously smelly, stinky lumps right by my paws. Inches from my nose and mouth. It was pure torture not to snatch them up, but I didn't. If Walter was trying to be part of our family-pack, he was going to have to work harder for it.

"I'd never try to take her from you, MahDi," he said. "I promise."

I gave it a little while before I ate them, just in case he checked in—I didn't want him to think I was too eager, or that I was giving him permission to make MomDoc pick him over me. That, I figured, is what Domino meant by working the humans.

That old cat sure knew a lot of good tricks because those were some of the best treats I'd ever had. And MomDoc never said a word when my belly reacted offensively on the car ride home.

CHAPTER 17

A few days later, we met Walter at the shelter so MomDoc could show him Koda. She thought they would make a good match, and I knew she was right. They'd be perfect for each other. A man with an empty heart and a dog looking for love.

They walked together through the kennel room, checking each pen.

"He was in this one yesterday," MomDoc said, pointing next to Leroi. "Weird. I know Huck said he was adopting some out. I wonder if he found him a home today."

Walter passed a cookie through the chain links to Leroi, then he stopped to give one to every other dog that came up to their gate. Sort of like at Halloween when MomDoc gave candy out to every kid who came up to the door. Only no funny clothes. Walter leaned close to a brown dog with big droopy eyes and a blunt tail down near Leroi.

"Aw, look at this guy, what's his story?"

MomDoc showed him the dog's card attached to the wall. "All the information we have is written here. Sometimes there isn't much."

I jogged past each kennel, looking inside for a sign of Koda. It wasn't just that we thought Koda was perfect for Walter; something told me Bailey would have picked him, too. And that was my obligation. But I didn't see him. Not until I got to the last kennel where he was stretched out on the concrete. A trickle of drool dribbled from his mouth to the floor.

Koda!

He opened one sad eye, but not even the very tip of his tail moved. Everything about him said the happy, grateful dog who'd crawled eagerly into the crate at the clinic after being discarded was gone. This new Koda felt rejected. Alone.

I slobbered on a lady. Guy made me come to the end so no one'll see me.

I ran in circles making enough noise to get MomDoc's and Walter's attention. Ozzie heard me, too, and raced in from the office.

Wut happened?

He skidded to a stop beside me and stared.

Oh-my-dog the heck you say, why he so sad?

Huck was mean about his slobber.

Koda sighed and closed his eye.

All I wanted wuz someone to love.

I knew that. Love was all over Koda, it had been from the time Toby and Beth came dragging him into the clinic. It wasn't too much to ask for.

Get up, Koda. Someone's here to meet you. Look sharp!

MomDoc looked into the kennel. "Wonder why he was moved all the way down here. And why is his water bowl bone dry?" She clenched her fists into tight balls. "I'm going to find Huck. He can't let this happen."

She stormed off down the aisle toward the office and Ozzie wagged his little tail.

Huck in trouble!

Walter put his face near the kennel and wiggled his fingers through the chain link. "Hey, fella, I hear great things about you."

Koda, hear that? He likes you, get up! Now!

He'll jus yell at me like they all do.

Ozzie put his front paws up against the wall and barked. From across the aisle, a short-haired senior dog paced in front of his gate.

If you don't wan' that home, I do.

The spaniel next to him barked.

Get up! Ya gotta look like ya want a family!

The very end of Koda's tail tapped on the floor. He raised his head and looked out at Walter.

Him?

Yes!!

Koda sat up and made that happy-happy-joy-joy-love sound and it was so obvious what he was saying, Walter didn't wait for MomDoc to come back. He opened the gate, slipped inside, and sat down on the concrete floor.

"Hey, boy, I'm Walter."

Koda flipped his tail on the ground, and then—I am not kidding you—that shaggy black dog sat up in front of Walter and smiled, just like a human. His lips stretched from one side of his face to the other, he squinted his eyes, and he made that *I love you so much* sound again that even humans understand. Walter reached both hands behind Koda's ears and the two of them stared into each other's eyes. Something magical was happening.

"You are something special," Walter said.

The senior dog across the aisle gave up when he heard that and lay down.

Better him than me I suppose.

The spaniel jumped up and down, his black ears flopping against his brown-and-white head.

Yeah! That's the way ya do it!

All throughout the room the shelter-friends watched and cheered Koda on.

It's happening!

      He's gettin' out!

            Oh my paws! He's gonna get a

home!

MomDoc came back without Huck and smiled that super-shiny way when she saw Walter inside with Koda. Ozzie ran in circles like he was celebrating, and I sat beside MomDoc, feeling that warmth come over me that happened every time we made a perfect match.

But then I smelled Huck and the whole mood changed. His big boots scraped against the floor and made a *scuff-scuff-scuff* sound all the way up the aisle. Huck was the only one not smiling. Koda flopped to the floor and hid his face behind Walter's leg.

      Don' let him see me!

Walter put his mouth near Koda's ear. "You don't need to be afraid with me here," he said quietly. He took a white cloth from his pocket and wiped some drool from the side of Koda's mouth.

"You comin' to take some of these dogs away?" Huck said too loud.

"I was just looking for you," MomDoc said. "We need to have a conversation about the dogs' water. This one's bowl was dry."

She pointed to Koda's pen.

"That dog slobbers so much, he don't need extra water. I

had a lady all ready to adopt and then he drooled all over her. She lit outta here like a bullet without taking an animal with her! If you ask me, this one ain't adoptable, anyway. He's just takin' up space. I found them orange tags in a drawer, we can slap one on his gate and call the—"

"No! Huck, what are you not understanding about this? All the other shelters are overflowing with too many dogs as it is. Sending him out means euthanasia, not adoption!"

"Hey, I'm the one in this place with them every single day, not you," Huck said. "There's too many of them making noise all the time, and now I've got this slobber-dog to contend with?"

MomDoc breathed in really deep one time, then blew a big puff of air out from her mouth. I went and sat next to her, leaning against her leg so she'd know I was there.

"I told you, Huck, I'm working on getting some temp foster homes," she said. "In the meantime, why don't you focus a little more diligently on potential adoptions. And look into the eyes of these dogs who need your help. Try to feel some empathy for them."

Huck's face turned dark again. He yanked the no-bite mitt off his hand and stalked away. He could try to fool anyone else, but we dogs knew. He was afraid of us. He hated working at the shelter and would do anything to make it easier until Mike came back. Even if it meant sending away perfectly perfect dogs in the white truck to The Unthinkable.

"He's so frustrating," MomDoc said to Walter after Huck was gone. "He's not an animal lover, and every time I see him he's wearing that no-bite mitt like he's expecting all of them to attack."

"I wouldn't blame them," Walter said. "He's not pleasant."

MomDoc rubbed her forehead. She was worried. I was worried. All the dogs in the shelter were worried. And they were quiet.

"I've got to find more foster homes, at least until Mike gets back."

Walter stroked Koda's side. "How does the problem get solved long term?"

"We've been hoping to organize a free spay-and-neuter clinic because that's where the problem starts—too many random litters of puppies who eventually find their way here."

"What happened to those plans?"

"Everything got put on hold when Mike went into the hospital."

Walter untangled a clump of hair in the scruff under Koda's neck. "Well, that's not good." He leaned close to Koda and talked quietly. "What if I told you I wanted you to come home with me?"

The tip of Koda's tail thumped on the ground.

"You understand *home*?"

Thump. Thump. Koda lifted his head from behind Walter's leg. He put one paw on his knee, then the other paw, and in one swift movement that shaggy black-and-white, slob-bering, bucket-of-love dog launched the entire front half of his body onto Walter's lap. He licked his face and made that sad-funny sound, something between a siren and a song that happens when there's too much joy for a dog to hold inside. Walter put both arms around his neck and buried his face in thick black fur.

We all went outside with Koda to test him with Walter and some of the dogs he hadn't played with yet. That's what always happened before anyone adopted a dog from the shel-ter, so the new family knew what to expect. Even with Huck ready to push any dog out the door whether they were right for a family or not, that's what we did. Because them's the rules.

Koda loved everyone. Everyone loved Koda. As it should be. Even Leroi, who wasn't much of a *play-with-me* dog and usually just sat by the fence waiting for Murph, was happy to see Koda and trotted up and down the yard while he bounced around and tried to get her to steal a rubber duck from his mouth. She finally wrestled it away and sat on top of it.

Not giving it up!

Walter laughed. "Hey, buddy, here, fetch!" He threw a ten-nis ball from the toy bin and Koda forgot about the rubber duck and went after it, then carried it back and dropped it at Walter's feet.

"You should know that Koda will likely need hip surgery

someday," MomDoc said.

Walter threw the ball across the yard again and shrugged. "That's fine, if it makes him feel better, that's what we'll do."

When Koda got tired, he sat beside Walter and leaned his head and shoulder against Walter's leg. A string of drool fell from the side of his mouth, but he looked up at Walter exactly the same way I'd looked at MomDoc that day when she'd rescued me. He was in love.

Finally, it was time for him to go to his new home. Koda pranced down that aisle for the last time with his tail wagging and his head high, looking side to side at everyone who'd come to say goodbye.

Good luck, buddy!

Happy for ya, man!

Bring us news from the outside!

Leroi sat wistfully at her gate.

Goodbye, Koda. If you find Murph, please let him know I'm still here.

Then she went back to her corner and lay down to wait.

CHAPTER 18

A few evenings later, I sat at the glass kitchen door watching Toby push the mower machine slowly back and forth across the backyard. He circled around the base of the aspen trees and ran the mower along the edge of the flower garden, past the hole Ozzie had dug right through the middle when he'd been sure there was an intruder hiding among the lilies.

Ozzie was scared of the mower machine and cowered under the table. He'd shaken so badly it made him throw up. Again. MomDoc crawled underneath to clean it up and knocked her head on the way out.

"Dang, bumping my head is as regular as you throwing

up, Oz. You'd think we'd both learn."

I turned back to look at him.

Chill out, buddy. We get elk meatballs tonight!

MomDoc liked to cook dinner for Toby when he helped her do things around the house. This time it was elk meatballs. Spicy sauce bubbled on the stove, and the aroma of roasting elk seeped from the oven where MomDoc had put them to cook. She stood at the kitchen counter shaving the stinkiest of stinky cheese into a bowl. Oh, the luscious smells of Toby-mowing-the-grass days.

Toby didn't like elk meatballs, but she didn't know that. So guess who got them? Yup. Me and Ozzie. Shhhh, it's a secret.

Beth was coming to dinner this time, too. Toby had said they had something important to tell MomDoc. After he put the mower machine away, he washed his hands in the sink and sat at the table. MomDoc lifted the lid off the big pot and stuck her nose up close. Because I have a super-sniffer instead of pockets, I didn't need to do that. I already knew that sauce was just right.

"School starts in a couple of weeks?" MomDoc asked.

"Yes, ma'am."

"Good, just in time for Mike to get back. I'm paying for kennel cleaners in the meantime so everything doesn't fall to you and Beth. Hopefully, that will help out some."

She stirred the sauce and put the lid back on the pot.

"Huck's just such a jerk," Toby said. "He reminds me of this kid on the bus who always pushes little kids out of their seats."

"Ugh. I know people like that. But I'm sure the second Mike gets here Huck will be out the door and never look back. We've got that to look forward to."

Ozzie sat up straight and wagged his tail.

She say no more Huck?

Soon.

Oh-my-dog, we gonna have a party?

He ran to the other room, grabbed his giant squeaky fish from the living room toy basket, dragged it all the way to the kitchen, and stomped on it to make it squeal.

Squeaky wants to party.

MomDoc tossed us each a sliver of super-stinky cheese. "You still want to be a vet after spending your summer working at the shelter?"

"Even more now. You always say the shelter problem starts with puppy mills and people not neutering their pets. I want to do something to change that."

"So ambitious, Toby, I'm impressed. You sure you're only thirteen?"

"Yes, ma'am, but that's actually why—"

MomDoc raised her hand. "Hey, Toby?"

"I know—don't say 'ma'am.' It's just hard because my dad says I have to."

"I don't see your dad here in my kitchen, do you? It will be our secret."

"Okay."

"Good. Dinner's just about done. When is Beth coming?"

Toby dropped his face to look at his phone but I could see his skin getting flushed. It's what always happened when he got embarrassed and Toby got embarrassed a lot. Especially when Beth was around.

"She's on her way now."

Dinner was about to happen! I gave Ozzie *The Look* and we met under the table.

Meatballs, comin' up?

Lip-smacking, yummiliscious, roasted elk meatballs.

He wagged his skinny tail and positioned himself by Toby's feet.

But it wasn't only Beth coming for dinner. Walter showed up, too, and walked right in like he *lived* here. I'd thought after Koda went home with him Walter might stop visiting so much, but no. Even worse, he brought Koda with him. No matter how happy I was to give Bailey his wish, and no matter how much Walter loved Koda and Koda loved him, he was *not* going to steal our elk meatballs!

MomDoc snapped a piece of paper towel off a roll and handed it to Walter. "For the slobber."

Gross.

Koda wiggled his body so hard when Walter wiped his

chin that his hind end banged against Beth's leg. *Bump. Bump. Bump.*

"Look at him!" Beth squealed, like Koda was the funniest, cutest, smartest dog ever. "You're so happy now!"

Koda rewarded Beth by doing that thing where he looked like he was human-smiling. His lips stretched side to side, he half closed his eyes, and his tail wagged obnoxiously hard.

Good grief.

Ozzie scooted close to me under the table.

Yeah, good grief.

Koda tried to break away from Walter to join us but I air-nipped at him.

Get back. Me and Ozzie only.

Elk meatballs were worth defending. So was our family-pack.

MomDoc got it. Not about the elk meatballs, she didn't know that part. But she knew it would take time before we were ready to accept Walter and Koda into our family. And with food around, fights could break out. She led Koda outside and put a bowl of kibble by the glass door, then she sprinkled some of the stinky cheese on top.

"Sorry, Koda, just for dinnertime."

Ozzie ran to the door and stared.

Why-the-heck he out there?

He was clueless that some of our meatballs could have ended up in Koda's mouth. 'Cuz Ozzie didn't think of those kinds of things. He was too nice. He was so nice his self-preservation radar was flawed. I barked sharply, just once, and he scrambled under the table again.

Sorry, Di.

Koda finished his dinner, then lay on the deck watching us through the glass. MomDoc sat down at her place.

"Help yourselves, everyone," she said.

We could hear them above us, passing around the bowl with the white stringy stuff called pasta, then the other one with the sauce and the meatballs. The whole room smelled like mouthwatering-deliciousness. Ozzie and I waited by Toby's feet. It would happen any second. Sure enough, Mom-Doc jumped up from the table.

"Oh no, I totally forgot milk. Toby? Beth? Either of you want milk?"

Ozzie and I stood, ready to pounce. Toby put his napkin in his lap.

"Sure," Beth said.

A single elk meatball rolled out of the napkin and dropped to the floor. I let Ozzie get the first one and I licked up the leftover juice. Koda pushed his nose against the door and whined.

Whatcha eatin' under there?

Don't look at him, Ozzie.

He moved over by Beth's feet, ready to swoop in for the kill if she saw what Toby had done and dropped hers for us, too.

"Darn, I forgot the cheese!" MomDoc said, jumping up again. "I'm such a scatterbrain tonight. We had really odd cases at the clinic today."

Another meatball tumbled from Toby's lap. I pounced on this one. Ozzie scarfed up the dribbles of sauce. No meatball coming down from Beth. MomDoc passed the bowl of super-stinky cheese and scooted her chair back to the table.

Plunk. There it went. The last meatball, right by Toby's feet.

But then, *Plunk.*

Another meatball dropped behind us—in front of *Walter's* feet. Ozzie and I stared at it. Walter's napkin drifted to the floor.

"Ooops," he said.

Then there he was, peering at us under the table with his finger to his lips. He winked, grabbed the napkin, and sat back up.

Ozzie and I scarfed them down while Koda watched pathetically through the glass, his head tilted to the side, his ears forward, and his tongue licking his lips. I didn't feel bad. It would be a long time before I relinquished those meatballs to anyone except Ozzie.

Domino meandered into the room and rubbed his body against the leg of the table, giving me his *I know best* look.

Don't be a sucker. Make him wait.

He was talking about Walter bribing us to accept him. I

was no dummy. I wasn't letting him into our pack that easily. Especially since it would be a package deal—Walter plus Koda. Not yet.

After dinner, Walter scooped ice cream into bowls and everyone went outside on the deck to eat it. Ozzie and I never got human ice cream, only the doggie cones at the drive-through store. I settled in the shade of Walter's chair. Domino sat on the kitchen window ledge, twitching his ear and watching for mice. Koda chased Ozzie under the peony bushes and around the aspen trees. They scrambled onto the deck, raced across the wood crashing into everyone's chairs, then dove off the other side.

And repeat.

Every time Koda got near, Walter stuck his hand out and grazed his fingers across his back.

"Such a happy boy."

"Hey, Doc," Toby said. "Beth and I wanted to talk to you about something."

This sounded serious. I sat up to watch Toby's face and listen for familiar words.

"Is everything okay?"

Beth smiled. "Oh yeah, it's just that back in my old town the vet did a free spay-and-neuter clinic a few times a year. Toby said you'd been planning one here before Mike got sick and I thought maybe we could help."

"A free spay-and-neuter clinic? I'll help!" Walter said.

"Aw, guys, that's really nice of you," MomDoc said. She was smiling really big. "The main obstacle is finding a location that can handle that volume of surgeries at one time."

"I know," Beth said. "Toby told me. That's where my mom comes in."

"Lydia?"

Lydia?

"Beth's mom is the new principal at our middle school," Toby said.

MomDoc sat up and raised her eyebrows. "Lydia is the principal?"

"Yeah. We used the high school gym for clinics back home," Beth said. "But since my mom is at the middle school here, I asked her if we could use it. I hope that's okay that I asked her before asking you."

"And what did she say?"

"Oh, she said yes, we could do it. It would have to be scheduled when no sports were happening, but there's lots of options."

"Wow, guys, this is amazing!"

"You two are real go-getters!!" Walter said.

I didn't know what a principal was, or a gymnasium, but what I did know was that Beth and Toby kept smiling at each other while they talked with MomDoc and Walter, and somehow Lydia had helped them plan a snip-snip clinic. Maybe she wasn't such a Grumpy-Pants after all.

Walter reached down and just barely touched the top of my head, then set his human ice cream bowl on the deck, right by my face. He scooted his chair over so MomDoc couldn't see that he'd given me his leftovers. And he'd done it in secret. I licked that bowl clean.

Later, when Toby and Beth were gone and the sun was setting behind the house, the tiny white lights MomDoc kept strung up around the deck flickered off and on. The sky was extra dark, no moon, and the blinking lights almost looked like flurries of snow. Ozzie was curled up in MomDoc's lap. Domino was sleeping on the windowsill. Koda was stretched out beside Walter, who kept one hand on Koda's side. The other hand reached for MomDoc's in the dark and we all stayed still like that for a while.

I knew what hand-holding meant. Walter was going to be around for some time. When it was time for him and Koda to leave, he reached down to pat me.

"I think maybe you're getting used to me, MahDi."

I closed my eyes and didn't move away. Maybe I would consider letting him be part of our family.

Maybe.

HOLLY

"Come on, Holly!"

Betsy pedals her bike down the road. Long pink ribbons fly off the handles. Her swimming clothes are in the basket—we're going to the lake!

I love the lake.

I love the water.

I love when Betsy throws the ball far away and I jump into the water and swim-swim-swim until I can grab it and bring it back to her. That makes Betsy laugh.

I live for Betsy's laugh.

She leans her bike against a tree and we run into the water to play. Afterward, I roll in the sand and scratch my back while Betsy eats her sammich. I'm not supposed to beg for food so I sit beside her and thump my tail against the ground. I don't look like I'm begging, but inside everything is saying:

Sammich!

Sammich!

Sammich!

Betsy hands me a bit of bread and meat. When she is done and I am almost dry she gets on her bike with the flying pink ribbons and I lope along beside her.

I love Betsy.

She pedals slowly going home. After she parks her bike in the garage, she leads me upstairs to her room.

"They're fighting again," she whispers. "Let's not listen."

She sits on the floor and puts the black cups over her ears so she only hears music. I can hear both music and Mom and Dad fighting. I lay my head on Betsy's leg and she ruffles my fur, then bends over and kisses me. Betsy knows I will always protect her.

Every day we go to the lake except when it is raining. Betsy puts a slicker over me and we go to the library instead. I have to wait outside. I don't mind. There is an overhang to keep rain from hitting me, and an old man with a walking stick gives me a treat from his pocket.

"My Lilah doesn't have a fancy raincoat like you, so she had to stay home today."

It is warm and drizzly and I doze under the shelter until Betsy comes back with new books. When we get home, Mom is happy. Stacks of newspaper are everywhere and lots of empty boxes.

"Dad got a new job!"

Betsy tenses. "What are the boxes for?"

"It comes with a house to live in. We're moving next week."

"Where?"

"Not far. Same school."

Betsy puts her hand on my collar. "What about Holly?"

Mom's face flashes something that makes me uneasy. "Don't worry, Holly will be fine. Take a couple of boxes and start packing up your room, okay?" Then she turns away.

Betsy takes boxes, a roll of tape, and a pair of scissors. "Come on, Holly."

"You want help?" Mom asks.

Betsy shakes her head. "It's not like I haven't done this a million times before."

I follow her upstairs and watch her tape the bottom and sides of the boxes and start throwing things inside.

"I'm sick of this, Holly. Last time they let me get you because they said we wouldn't move anymore and now look."

She kneels in front of me and wraps her arms around my neck. I lean against her.

I will always be with you.

I will always protect you.

I will never let anything bad happen to you.

Every afternoon we go to the lake, but Betsy doesn't swim anymore. She sits on a log and pokes a stick in the sand and makes shapes. I look for the ball but she doesn't bring it. I run to the edge of the water and bark for her to follow. She smiles for a second, then draws another shape. I trot back and she scratches behind my ears.

I understand. She needs me to stay beside her. Not play, not swim, not chase balls—just be with her.

So I do.

At home, Mom and Dad pack things into boxes. When they are done, Mom says the movers are coming.

"Go to the lake. Here's five dollars to get ice cream. Take your time."

She leans down and mouths some words to me I don't understand, then wipes her eyes with the back of her hand. A big van is outside and people have come to move the boxes and furniture. Everything is ready to go except that my bed, my bowls, and my toys are stacked in a pile in the kitchen. My food is on the counter.

I don't know what this means.

When we get back, everything is out of the house and inside the big van. Mom tells Betsy I have to stay behind for now, that they will come back for me.

"She'll be in the way and might get hurt."

Once Betsy is in the car, Mom runs back inside, takes

my face in her hand, and looks me in the eye. "I'm so sorry, Holly. Someone will come for you later. You've been such a good girl."

Then she puts a paper on the counter and leaves.

I stand by the front window where I've always waited for Betsy to come home from school and I watch them drive away. Betsy is looking at me, but she's not smiling. No one is.

I know the truth.

They won't come back.

Betsy is gone.

There is no one to protect her.

I finish the bowl of dog food long before anyone comes. I drink water from the toilet and go outside through the doggie door to relieve myself, but there is a pile of poop by the fence that no one has cleaned up. Two pink ribbons from Betsy's bike floated into the yard and are stuck in the branches of a tree.

Day after day I sit by the front window, waiting. At night, when thunder makes the house rumble, I dig my teeth into the living room carpet and rip a hole the size of my head. Soon, I've gone through the carpet in every room and scratched the wood of every door. I've licked my side until the hair has come off my flank, leaving a raw, red circle as big as my paw, and I am starving.

Finally, one day two men come in, one tall, one short. The tall one waves his hand in front of his nose and the short man wrinkles his face.

"What's that smell?"

The short man sees me cowering. I know I am in trouble, but his face softens and he kneels before me.

"Poor thing is so scared it's shaking," he says.

"There's a note on the counter," the tall man says. "About the dog."

The letter tells them my name is Holly, that I am two years old and I belonged to Betsy. "She has been well loved. Please find her a good home. Thank you."

"They left her for five days with a *note*?"

The short man's tone has turned angry and I shake. He sounds like Dad. I nip at my leg and lick some loose hair off the skin.

The tall man goes off down the hall, then sprints up the stairs. He will see what I have done to the carpets. I push myself against the wall and try to disappear. When he comes back, I close my eyes.

"Carpet torn up everywhere," he says. "It'll have to be replaced."

The short man touches the back of my neck very carefully. "You're not in trouble," he says.

"We should report those people," the tall man says. "They should be fined for animal abuse."

I don't know what they mean, but they put a handful of food in my bowl and fill the other with water. I scarf the kibble up. Just as fast, it ends up in a wet pile on the kitchen floor.

"What do we do with her?" the tall man asks.

"The shelter in town had a fire a few weeks ago, can't take her there. I'll take her home for now," the short man says. "This is pathetic."

He lifts me in his arms and carries me out and lays me gently on the back seat of his car. I sit up and watch as the tall man closes the door to our home. The last thing I see as we drive away is another pink ribbon from Betsy's bike draped on a bush in the yard.

They took the bike instead of me.

CHAPTER 19

MomDoc put her suitcase by the front door. Me and Ozzie and Domino were lined up side by side, waiting for her to tell us which one got to come for whatever trip she was taking. A suitcase is a dead giveaway.

"I need to get my eyes on Auntie, guys, and be sure she's okay in her new home. I just have this feeling something is wrong."

Domino heard *Auntie* and stood up, stretched, then went to sit in front of the door as if that was the signal he was going. MomDoc picked him up and moved him next to Ozzie.

"Sorry, Domino, not this time."

Then she was gone and the three of us jumped onto the

back of the sofa to watch her drive away, but she didn't look back and wave like she normally would. Something must have been seriously wrong.

Domino stalked around the house all morning, hissing, meowing, scratching the bottom of the couch—which he knew he was never, ever supposed to do, but he did, anyway. Ozzie tried to push him away.

You're gonna get in trouble, stop!

Domino arched his back and swatted at him.

Get away, tattletale, I'll do what I want.

He prowled about for a bit, making a lot of noise, then went upstairs to MomDoc's bed and slept for the rest of the day.

She hadn't said anything about who would be staying overnight to take care of us like usual, but a little before lunchtime Toby and Beth rode up to the house on their bikes. Ozzie zoomed from the sofa to the door.

I call Beth!

This time I got the wicker basket and when we rode past Lilah's house I sat up tall, hoping she'd see me in my fancy seat. Ozzie kept turning around in the doggie-pack and almost fell out twice so we had to stop. Beth was buckling him in tighter when a squirrel darted across someone's lawn. Ozzie wriggled and squirmed and whined and yipped in her face.

Oh-my-dog, don' you know there's a squirrel?

Chill, Ozzie, we have work to do at the shelter!

Oof, the heck you say . . .

He sank down into the doggie-pack and pouted the rest of the way there.

In the kennel room, Huck was backed into the corner of Leroi's pen with a leash in one hand and the giant bite-proof mitt on the other. Leroi was stretched out on her bed, watching him. No growling. No threat. No reason for the mitt.

"Come on, Scrounge-Rat, let me put this thing on," Huck said. He took one tiny step toward Leroi. "If you bite me, it's doomsday for you."

Leroi didn't flinch. I wanted to go to her, but Toby flicked his hand downward, telling me to wait. Beth picked Ozzie up in her arms and held his muzzle so he couldn't bark. They wanted to see what Huck was up to before he saw us. But Leroi caught our scent. She raised herself up off the bed, and Huck threw himself backward into the corner, screaming.

"Get away, you mongrel!"

Leroi trotted past without even looking at Huck cowering, pushed the gate open with her nose, and came to sit beside us.

Where's Mike? Murph can't call with no

Mike!

I licked her face and wagged my tail. Leroi was a good dog.

Back soon.

Huck threw the leash to the floor and stormed out of the

kennel. His face looked like a wet balloon, dripping with sweat and ready to pop. He flailed his arms around.

"I'm done! That's it! You saw that dog. She tried to bite me!"

He didn't give anyone a chance to say anything before he marched past, his fists bunched tight. Beth and Toby both giggled once he was out of the room.

"That went well," Beth said.

"At least he was embarrassed that we saw him being so dumb," Toby said. "I'm going to check on Hickory."

Beth let Leroi stay out of her kennel and follow her around while she gathered water bowls and took them to the sink to wash. I started down the aisle, checking on everyone. The spaniel was gone and so was the husky and one other from the fire rescue, but there was a new dog, a brown-and-black cattle dog with flecks of white throughout her thick coat and a white butterfly spot on her forehead. She got up and came over to sniff.

Where's Marilease?

I didn't know Marilease, but I knew this story too well and never had the right answer when a new dog asked for the humans they were missing. So, sometimes, I lied.

MomDoc will find her.

Stuffy, too?

Stuffy, too.

I moved on to the next dog, and the next, and the next,

until I got all the way to the end.

Toby came back leading Hickory on a leash. "His leg seems like it's a lot better," he said. "Let's take him out back so he can feel the grass under his feet."

"Okay if I bring this little cattle dog? It says her name is Quinn and she's nine, so she's probably quiet. Leroi wants to come, too, and I'm guessing MahDi because he is clinging to my legs," Beth said.

A few minutes later, me and Beth and Toby were out in the play yard with Hickory, Leroi, and Quinn. Beth was right, Quinn quietly went about her business, relieving herself in a far corner, then sitting beside Leroi at the fence and looking out to the road. Leroi sniffed Quinn's ear.

I'm watching for Murph.

Quinn scooted a little closer to the fence.

Is this where we wait for people?

This is where we wait.

Quinn turned her face to the road and the two of them sat side by side, studying the cars that drove by. Behind them, Hickory limped to the corner to take care of business, then wandered around sniffing and pushing the bottom of the fence, looking for a weak spot to escape. I trotted over to him.

You're okay here.

His blue eyes paled so much in the sunlight they looked almost like snow at nighttime.

How do you know?

I turned to my side so he could see where The Spare used to be.

MomDoc fixed me. She'll fix you all the way, too.

Hickory wasn't interested in my missing spare. He found a patch of soft, clean grass and stretched out in the sun. Toby and Beth stood by the door. Beth pushed the screen on her phone and held it up for Toby to hear the music coming from inside. I sat down in the sun so I could enjoy the peace and quiet for a minute because, at a shelter, who knew how long that could last?

Not long. Beth had just changed the music when I heard Ozzie scratching and barking from the other side of the door.

Let me out! Let me out!

Beth pushed the handle, but the door wouldn't open.

"Oh no, it's locked!" Beth said. "We can't get back in!"

"Yes we can," Toby said. "Watch this secret trick Mike showed me when I got locked out once."

He moved the wooden toy bin over near the door and climbed up on top of it.

"If you ever get stuck out here, there's a safety rope that unlatches the lock inside. It's much easier than climbing that chain-link fence and almost killing yourself getting over the top."

He braced himself against the wall and reached up high,

grabbed a piece of rope that was hanging down under the eaves, and yanked. The door swung open on its own. Toby jumped down.

"Voilà!" he said, smiling.

Beth giggled again. I loved it when she did that. Her whole face shined. "I wonder how many times Mike got locked out before he put that string up there."

"I don't know, but I've had to use it a bunch so I'm glad he did," Toby said.

Ozzie ran outside dragging a ragged stuffed toy with a patched place above one eye.

Hey! Guys! Look wut I found!

Quinn bolted from the fence so fast she was a blur, speeding across the yard.

Stuffy!

She snatched the toy from Ozzie's mouth before he knew what had happened and sprinted around the yard. Ozzie chased after her, pumping his mini-pistons across the ground, but even as an old lady Quinn was faster than most any dog I'd ever seen. There was no way he was going to catch her.

Hey! I found it!

Leroi loped in a circle near the center of the yard and even Hickory sat up to watch Quinn hurtle past. After a bunch of trips around the yard, Quinn jerked to a stop, dropped the toy by her feet, and lay down on top of it.

My Stuffy!

Ozzie panted beside her, his little head tilted.

It wuz in the trash.

Quinn tucked Stuffy farther under her belly.

The bad man took her from me. She smells like Marilease.

Ozzie stood beside her, eyeing the toy, until Toby rolled a ball from the toy bin across the grass to distract him.

"Look, Oz! Get it!"

The fuzzy yellow ball bounced over bumps in the earth and Ozzie was off, chasing it down and bringing it back to Toby to throw again. After a few rounds, while Leroi and Quinn rested up, and Hickory wandered over for a sniff of Stuffy, Beth threw a bright-colored Frisbee through the air.

"Look up!"

The Frisbee soared almost as high as the top of the building and hovered in a puff of wind, then floated slowly toward the earth. Ozzie ran underneath it, jumping up and down.

I gots it, I gots it!

That Frisbee was still as high as the fence when Quinn launched herself into the air with her front legs tucked tight. She grabbed it in her teeth and landed like she'd been doing that trick her whole life. Then she limped over to Beth and dropped the Frisbee at her feet.

CHAPTER 20

Domino was still stalking around the house meowing and hissing when MomDoc got back the next day. As soon as he heard her car pull up out front, he jumped on the chair by the TV table, curled into a tight ball, and pretended to be asleep. I mean let's be real, MomDoc knew exactly how Domino would act when she didn't take him to Auntie's. But this time, she came home with a surprise for him. Auntie was moving in!

We didn't get much of a chance to clamber all over her because Walter and Koda showed up right away. Almost like he'd been watching from some secret spot until he saw her car coming up the road so he could swoop in and take over.

He made two trips from MomDoc's car, then unloaded a bag of groceries onto the kitchen counter. The whole time, wherever he moved, Koda stayed so close to Walter it was like he was stuck with that fancy glue. His tail was tucked and his head low.

"What's wrong with him?" MomDoc asked.

Walter took a package of beefsteaks out of the grocery bag and put them on the counter. How do I know they were beefsteaks when I couldn't see the top of the counter? That super-sniffer of mine.

"I don't know. We were at the store and a truck went by with a kid hanging half his body out the window waving at me and yelling 'Wilson!' He must have mistaken me for someone else, but Koda started shaking and climbed onto my lap when we got in the car. No idea what that was about."

"These dogs and their vehicle fears. MahDi is terrified of white trucks, always has been but I've never known why. Something in his history."

I reached down and nipped the top of my paw. I hated that white truck. I hated the memory of the white truck in my life before and after the accident, and I hated that now it meant sending dogs off for The Unthinkable. I'd never not hate a white truck.

Beth and Toby came over just a little bit after MomDoc and Walter got home. Beth was pushing one of those things on wheels that little kids sit in.

"Is it okay that Andrew comes in? I had to babysit," she said.

Andrew! The baby? I trotted over to sniff him out, expecting something ugly and awful after all the crying we heard when they first moved in, but there was nothing wretched about him. Andrew's head was covered with thick yellow hair. He had big blue eyes and his cheeks were flushed with rosy spots, and he clutched the edge of a blanket in his chubby hands. He even smelled clean, like powder and shampoo, and he giggled when he saw me.

"Dog!"

Beth parked his buggy in a corner of the kitchen and handed him a rubber donut.

"He'll be quiet with his blankie and a teething toy," she said. He squealed a happy noise and gummed the donut in his mouth. Ozzie positioned himself right by the side of the buggy.

I'ma get that toy when he drops it, jus you
wait 'n' see.

Everyone was talking at the same time. Toby was telling MomDoc about Hickory, Beth was trying to talk over him and tell her about the new dog, Quinn. Walter was trying to coax Koda outside so he could get to the grill without tripping over him, and Domino had finally given up pretending like he didn't care that MomDoc was home and strutted back and forth on top of the kitchen table, demanding attention.

Loudly. The only one besides me who wasn't causing a fuss was the baby.

And then the doorbell rang.

"Oh, it's probably my mom," Beth said.

Ozzie and I ran ahead, but it wasn't Lydia. It was Lucy, standing on the step with her dad, who was holding Mademoiselle's fishbowl in his arms. Mademoiselle herself was floating on top of the water, upside down, as dead as any goldfish I'd ever seen.

"Oh!" Beth said.

MomDoc saw Lucy and the goldfish bowl. "Oh!"

Lucy hiccupped. Her cheeks were wet from tears. "Mademoiselle died! I need to know *why*!"

"Sorry to barge in like this, Lucy insisted we come over for you to see Mademoiselle right away," the dad said.

Lucy didn't have gloves or a mask on, so I nipped at Ozzie.

Stay back. Allergies.

Domino watched from the stairs, his ears twitching and his one eye pinned on dead Mademoiselle. I moved toward him.

Don't you even . . .

He arched his back and hissed.

A guy can dream, okay?

MomDoc kneeled in front of Lucy. "I am so sorry. You took such good care of her, better than any other goldfish person I've ever known. It wasn't anything you did."

Lucy hiccupped again. "Then why?"

"I'm not sure, Lucy. You've had her for several years and we don't know how old she was when you got her. It could just be old age."

Lucy looked up at the bowl where Mademoiselle had lived such a happy life with her green and blue gravel and her plant from Africa.

"I don't want her to die. A hundred bazillion times I don't want that!"

Her dad smoothed the hair on top of her head and his face softened. "Did you hear that, sweetie? You were the best goldfish owner Doc's ever known."

Lucy sniffled and her yellow pigtails bobbed. "I don't know what to do now," she said in a teeny, tiny voice.

MomDoc took Lucy's hands in hers. "This is the part where you grieve. You can bury her, then do something special to remember Mademoiselle. You will feel sad for a while, and you'll always love her, but I bet that someday you'll be ready to find another goldfish to love so Mademoiselle will see from goldfish-heaven that you're happy again. Because you know that's what she would want."

Lucy leaned her forehead against MomDoc's chest and sighed. "Do you think she knew I loved her?"

"Yes, Lucy, a hundred bazillion times I know that for a fact."

Everyone was quieter after Lucy left. I didn't know for

sure that goldfish went over the same Rainbow Bridge as dogs and cats and guinea pigs and chinchillas, but MomDoc had said *goldfish-heaven* and I would bet a hundred bazillion liver treats that it was filled with plants from Africa for Mademoiselle to hide in.

The next morning, MomDoc and Walter were drinking coffee on the deck and talking about Auntie moving in when the doorbell rang again. Koda and Ozzie had been racing around the backyard, kicking up enough dirt to make a cloud in the air, but when that bell rang, we all went to see who was there. It was no one. Or, it had been someone and they left behind a bright orange envelope on the step that smelled like Lucy. Like candy-on-a-stick.

MomDoc opened the envelope. "It's an invitation."

"To what?" Walter asked.

"Mademoiselle's funeral."

"Oh, how incredibly sweet. What does it say?"

"Please join us to celebrate the remarkable life of Mademoiselle next Thursday at five o'clock in the afternoon. We will have French pastries, listen to Mademoiselle's favorite Edith Piaf songs, and share stories of our dearly departed friend."

"French pastries and Edith Piaf, that sounds like the perfect way to memorialize a fancy goldfish," Walter said.

"I'd expect nothing less."

The rest of the day was taken up with MomDoc and Walter moving things out of the spare room downstairs and bringing in the bed and dresser and rug from the guest room upstairs. It was a lot of up and down and heaving and grunting, but we were all excited that Auntie was coming to live with us.

"I hope this is the right thing," MomDoc said. "She's so unhappy in assisted living and I feel an obligation to her."

"It is definitely the right thing," Walter said. "Besides, Domino would be upset if you changed your mind now."

As soon as the bed was moved and made up, and MomDoc laid some of Auntie's clothes on top, Domino claimed it for his own. He stretched and made biscuits with his paws in one of Auntie's sweaters, then curled into a tight ball and fell asleep.

Ozzie had never seen Auntie. The only thing he knew about her was that she loved having Domino sit in her lap. He ran back and forth from all the toy baskets around the house gathering up stuffed animals and hiding them under her bed. When he was done, he crawled underneath and inspected his loot, then came back out, tail wagging.

Everthin's ready!

"When will she come?" Walter asked.

"I'm going back Thursday and will do the paperwork with the facility and doctors on Friday. Saturday I'll pack everything up and get ready for the movers. We'll be back on Sunday, and on Monday the home health nurse will start coming every day."

"How can I help?"

I went off to my living room bed for a nap and to ponder this change. It wasn't just going to be Auntie moving in, but someone else would be coming and going every day, too. A home health nurse. What if we didn't like her?

So many new things in such a short time. I fell asleep thinking about how it used to be with Mike and Rebecca at the shelter and no Huck. Before Walter came along and brought Koda over with him. When Toby was the only kid who hung around the house. Don't get me wrong, Beth was good and Toby was happier with her at the shelter, but everything was more predictable before all the changes. It was what I'd gotten used to.

Then there was the whole part about the fire at the other shelter and all the extra dogs that had to come to ours and worrying about finding them good homes, like we did with Tootsie and Mrs. Comfort, or Koda and Walter, and the whole thing about how too many dogs made Huck nervous and angry. It was all so unsettling, and I wondered when things might go back to normal. If they ever did.

CHAPTER 21

fter the clinic work on Monday, we dropped Ozzie off at home and went to pick out bouquets for the families who had sent their friends over the Rainbow Bridge the week before. I loved the flower shop. They kept a jar of cookies in the back for me, plus there were always so many different fragrances. Nothing like the store-of-many-smells that smelled like gasoline and MomDoc's morning coffee.

MomDoc pulled a handful of flowers from buckets and held them out for me to see. "I think Story's family will like these. I know you can't tell, but if you put the red and yellow flowers together they kind of look like the color of his coat."

Story had lived for a while after they discovered the

tumors, but the day they brought him in to say goodbye was one of the saddest ever for me. His family would love anything that reminded them of the big furry dog. Especially the kids who watched TV lying curled up next to him on the floor and rode him around like a pony. He was a gentle giant until he thought one of those kids was being threatened. Then, all the rules changed. We'd find just the right dog for them, I knew that for sure.

The girl put the flowers into a vase while MomDoc picked out a bouquet for Lucy.

"Green and blue like the gravel in her bowl, and some bright orange, I think, right, Di? Something feathery."

There were two other families to get flowers for and, after the girl who worked at the store made sure I had enough cookies, we drove off. My job on these errands was to bring comfort. That meant playing with kids if that's what was needed, like at Story's house. At least until the smallest boy tried to sit on me and cried when I couldn't move, even after he yelled "Giddyup!"

Sometimes it meant just sitting quietly beside someone and letting them pat my head. Hands-on-animals equaled comfort most of the time. I went inside with MomDoc to visit every family until we got to Lucy's. She lived in the neighborhood behind ours, in a house that looked a lot like Mr. Crandle's, so it wasn't hard to pick out. Especially since a giant-sized, bright orange fish-shaped balloon floated above the fence by the yard.

"Oh," MomDoc said. "How sweet. Someday I'm going to convince that mom to let Lucy have a hypoallergenic dog. But in the meantime, you wait here, I won't be long."

MomDoc came out the front door a few minutes later and Lucy stood in her front yard waving to me.

"I sent treats!" she called. Then she blew me a kiss and went inside.

We were almost home when Huck called MomDoc on the phone.

"You're on speaker, Huck, but it's just me and MahDi, what's up?"

"The feed delivery guy left the door open when I was logging a new dog in and it bolted. Gone! And I don't have the time to go find it!"

"Where are Toby and Beth?"

"Out doing dumb kid stuff, I guess. All I know is they ain't here, it's just me and the cleaners."

"Okay, I'm out in the car now, tell me about the dog and I'll look for it."

"Female, some kinda retriever-looking mix, hot-pink collar, really skinny. Guy said she'd been left behind when some people moved. Name was Noelle or Holly or something. I wrote it down somewhere. I gotta go, all kinds of drama over here."

MomDoc disconnected the call. "Holy smokes, MahDi,

Huck must be really terrified of dogs to make him act that way. Keep your eye out for a scared retriever with a pink collar."

Keep your eye out meant a dog had gone off somewhere. I watched out the window while we drove around, but the only dogs we saw were on leashes and we searched everywhere. No trace.

Later, MomDoc had our dinner bowls lined up on the kitchen counter and was dishing up supper when Toby and Beth rode up on their bikes leading a golden retriever with her tail tucked between her legs.

"We were leaving the lake and saw her grab someone's sandwich right out of their hand!" Beth said. "She wouldn't go near anyone except me. Her tag says her name is Holly but the phone number is disconnected."

Holly had long hair and dark eyes that darted everywhere. Her tail was so far under her body I thought it would stick there forever. It had been a while since she'd had anything to wag about.

"We called Huck's cell but he was gone and said she'd have to stay in the drop pen overnight because the shelter was closed," Toby said. "We didn't know what else to do."

MomDoc motioned them in. Holly kept her head flush up against Beth's leg. She wouldn't look at me.

"I know about her," MomDoc said. She kneeled in front of Holly and checked her over. "She got loose when Huck was doing an intake and he was all kinds of frazzled. She can stay here for tonight. I'll take her back in the morning."

Toby and MomDoc went to get one of the extra crates from the garage to clean it out. Beth sat on the living room floor, stroking Holly's head in her lap.

"You're so pretty," she said. "Is someone missing you?"

Holly closed her eyes and her tail tap-tap-tapped on the floor. Ozzie got close and sniffed her all over.

She sad.

I know.

I make her happy.

He ran to Auntie's new room and came back dragging Yellow Duck across the floor and pushed it up beside her.

Fur you.

Holly tucked Yellow Duck a little closer, then put her head back in Beth's lap and sighed.

"I wish I could take you home," Beth said. "But Mom says we aren't quite ready."

That night, when Holly's crate was set up next to my kitchen bed, MomDoc tried to get her to go inside but Holly locked her legs and whined.

"It's just for one night," MomDoc said.

Ozzie climbed inside.

Is ok in here.

Holly still wouldn't budge, not even when MomDoc tossed some treats into the back. A trickle of yellow pee seeped out from underneath her back end, wetting the long feathery hairs under her tail. She hung her head and looked at me.

Please no.

I nudged the gate closed and sat in front, blocking it.

"Okay, guys, I can take a hint," MomDoc said. She brought a clean bed and set it on the floor between mine and Ozzie's, then sent us out to the backyard. "I'm going to latch the doggie doors for the night, so everybody get your business done now."

Ozzie danced around Holly until she would play with him. He showed her his favorite toy-hiding spots and let her dig up a half-buried bone in the garden to keep. She trotted around behind him with that bone in her mouth like she'd won some kind of prize. MomDoc sat on the edge of the deck and pulled me up next to her.

"Imagine leaving your dog alone when you move away," she said. "It makes me feel even better about Auntie coming to live with us."

I lay down and put my chin on her thigh, watching the little white lights around the deck twinkle, and listening to Ozzie and Holly run around the yard together. There were so many things about humans that I didn't understand—dogs being abandoned was just one. But the most confusing part was that I knew Holly had been loved before she'd been discarded. No matter how hard I tried to figure that out, I couldn't make the two things go together.

The next morning, Holly was gone. I ran through the house searching for her. I checked the bathroom, the dining room, the living room, behind the couch, and under the TV table. Nothing. The only doggie door that was left unlatched went from the laundry room to the garage, but she wasn't out there, either.

MomDoc wasn't going to be happy, but I had to wake her up. If Holly had gotten out somehow, there was no telling how far she could have run. Or who might have grabbed her off the street. The uncertainty made my belly hurt.

All that worry was for nothing. Holly was curled up on MomDoc's bed, squished between her and Ozzie. She raised her head and looked at me standing in the doorway.

Just like with Betsy.

Then she snuggled in and closed her eyes, safe and happy and, for right now, loved. As it should be for all the dogs everywhere.

I went downstairs to the living room and climbed onto the back of the sofa to watch the light outside change as the sun rose again for another day.

CHAPTER 22

W hat the heck?" MomDoc read the sign stuck to the shelter door out loud. "No intake, no adoptions? What is Huck doing?"

At that moment, he was lounging in Rebecca's chair with his big feet propped up on the desk, tossing the no-bite mitt from one hand to the other.

"I'll tell you what I'm doing," he said when MomDoc asked about the sign. "Those kids who help start school next week. Mike may or may not be back by then, so that leaves just me and the cleaners." He sat up and slapped the mitt down on the desk. "Something has to give, and it ain't gonna be me."

"If you don't do adoptions, none of the dogs will get moved

out. That just makes it harder."

Huck had a wild look in his eyes. I moved closer to Mom-Doc and kept watch on every move he made.

"Look, do you know how many I've done where the people bring the dog back after I've filled their kennel with something else? It's not a rotating door; once they go they should stay gone. Besides, I cleared out most of them dogs that came from the fire by myself!"

MomDoc was getting frustrated and it showed. She took a deep breath before she answered him. "I think if you were more careful about screening potential adopters you could make better matches, and they would stay with their new families and not come back."

Huck's eyes flashed.

"Whatever. I didn't sign up for all this, I'm only staying 'cuz it looks bad for my cop training if I quit. If some yoyo walks in and says he likes a dog, he gets the dog. Besides, the guy from the state said I am acting manager and I make the decisions for now. Unless you want me to make a list and call the guy to come pick a bunch of them up, that's how it's gotta be."

This was the first time I felt MomDoc's anger at Huck do more than just simmer. I mean, even a patient person can only hold back for so long. She propped her fists on the desk and leaned toward him.

"No, I do not want you making a list, that isn't the way to

solve the problem, Huck. We're in the business of rescuing animals, not eliminating them." She pushed the no-bite mitt across the desk. "And you don't need to wear this all the time. You just have to be nice to the animals. They'll return the favor."

"These dogs don't like me. Feeling's mutual, but I'm not willing to get bit just because some white knight might come along next week or next month and take them off my hands. Like this one. Give her to me, I'll take her back."

I almost growled when he took Holly's leash, but I didn't because MomDoc wouldn't like that, even though Huck deserved more than just a growl. Like a big ol' bite in the back of his big ol' pants.

Holly tucked her tail when Huck led her off.

Help me.

We'll be back!

It was the best I could do.

MomDoc sat in the car for a second before we left, staring at the sign on the door. I knew that look. She was thinking. Pondering. Then she got out of the car, marched up the steps, and yanked it off.

"Ninety-nine percent of the time they aren't going to bite if they feel safe," she mumbled as we drove away.

Walter was going to stay with us at night while MomDoc was gone to get Auntie, but Toby was in charge of us during the day. Which meant we'd be able to check on the shelter-friends even though MomDoc was gone.

"Toby's dad felt four straight days and nights is too much for him alone," MomDoc told Walter. "Besides, I'm sure he and Beth have plenty to do before school starts up next Tuesday."

On Thursday morning, me and Ozzie and Domino all lined up on the sofa and watched her drive away. She turned to wave, then put her fingers to her lips and blew us a kiss. "Be good!"

Ozzie tried to climb higher on the back of the sofa and pushed Domino aside.

Hey, watch it, junior!

Sorry-sorry-sorry, aren't you so excited!

Auntie's comin' to stay!

Domino went off to the new downstairs bedroom for a nap while Ozzie and I waited for Toby to come get us.

The sign was back on the door of the shelter when we rode up on the bikes. I don't know if it said the same thing as before because neither Toby nor Beth read the words out loud. Huck was in Rebecca's chair again with his stinky, bunion-feet propped on her desk. He shoved some papers into an open drawer and stood up quickly.

"I thought you had to go to a funeral," he said. He turned a pad of paper over on the desk and put his hand on top like he didn't want anyone to see it.

"We do," Toby said. "But we're here to help first."

Huck plopped back down in the chair. "Whatever. Who died?"

"Mademoiselle, a goldfish," Toby said.

Pause . . .

Huck scoffed. "Are you serious? You're going to a funeral for a goldfish?"

"What about it?" Toby said. His face was getting flushed. "It's for a little girl, one of Doc's clients."

Huck laughed and threw his hands up. "You people are a trip, no lie, you'd be laughed out of town if you ever thought about setting up shop somewhere else."

I hated the way he talked to Beth and Toby when Mom-Doc wasn't around. The beginning of a growl vibrated in my throat, but Toby snapped his fingers at me behind his back. *Don't!*

"Maybe that's why we're here and you're there," Beth said.

Huck flipped his hand at her. "Yeah, I'm right here sittin' in the manager's chair, not you. Go clean up poop."

I'd had enough. I went to the door to the kennel room and scratched.

"Your buddy there wants to go stare at all the inmates. Let him through, would you? I'm busy." He tilted his head back like he was going to take a nap. "Oh, but one more thing. Don't take that sign off the door again. I had two people sneak dogs in after your vet friend took it down. I'm done.

No more. Nada. Got it? Or else the lot of them go off in the white truck."

"Sure, Huck, whatever you say," Beth said.

Squirt, the little Havanese MomDoc had saved from heat-stroke was in the kennel next to Quinn now. She jumped up and down on a cushy bed.

Hey! Hey! It's me! It's me!

A ribbon tied on top of her head had come loose and flopped over one eye. Ozzie ran on his mini-pistons and skidded to a stop in front of her.

Oh-my-dog, why you here?

Beth walked by leading Quinn outside, and smiled at Squirt. "I'll be right back for you."

Where's Allison?

Squirt got quiet and sat down. I knew right away what had happened before she even told us. Allison had done the right thing. Only the timing couldn't have been worse.

She wants me to have a good home where I don' hide.

Ozzie stood on his back legs and put his front paws against Squirt's gate.

Don' you worry. MahDi get you a good home!

Squirt splayed her legs out and lay on the floor.

I only wan' Allison.

Beth came back and read the tag posted on Squirt's kennel.

"Owner relinquish. Breed: Havanese. Approximate age: three. Housebroken: yes. Weight: ten pounds. Awwww." She crouched next to Squirt and gave her a good belly rub. "I'd live in the streets before I'd give up a dog I loved. Come on, you can play with Quinn and Holly. They'll show you the ropes."

Ozzie followed Beth and Squirt out to the play yard, and I made my way down the aisle to check on the other dogs. A tiny papillon with butterfly ears was sitting on a round plush cushion in a kennel. She perked up when she saw me sniffing around.

I'm Penelope. I'm waiting for Lillian to come back.

On the other side of Penelope was a sweet boxer-collie mix with a sparkle in his eye. He bounded over to the gate and sniffed, his whole body wagging.

Hi! Hi! Hi! I'm Bear, who are you? Can we play?

Soon.

Bear sat down to wait with a one-armed monkey toy in his mouth, and I moved on. The fella in the last kennel lay so still on his side that I had to check to be sure he was breathing. His body rose and fell but his eyes stayed closed. He was big and white with a curled tail, and he smelled strangely familiar. I pawed at his gate. Nothing. What was that scent I picked up? I pawed again and whined.

Do I know you?

He shifted ever so slightly and when he did I knew what it was. Sheep! I smelled sheep! It was Hero, the dog from the ranch with the dead lamb. That ranch lady had dumped him, even though MomDoc said she would find him a home.

Hero. Look up. It's me.

He opened an eye and his nose twitched.

I'm useless.

I sat near him for a good while, but his heart was so sad, he didn't really care who was there. He'd had the wrong job, that was all. He needed a family with kids to protect and a big place to run. Then he'd be happy and useful at the same time.

Toby and Beth came and went, switching out dogs to go in small groups for playtime. Later, when all the shelter-friends were resting in their pens, and Toby and Beth were refilling water bowls and replacing dirty blankets with clean ones, Huck came in and yelled down the aisle.

"Don't you have some goldfish funeral to go to?"

He didn't wait for an answer, he just laughed and closed the door.

Beth narrowed her eyes. "He makes me so mad."

"I know, but Doc says ignore him," Toby said. "Once Mike is back, then everything will be so much better. And he's right, we do need to get to Lucy's house. It's almost time."

It was hard leaving the shelter-friends that day. I stopped

by Leroi's kennel on the way out to check on her. She was lying on her bed, her ears flopping against her neck, looking sad and frightened.

We'll be back. Everything will be okay.

She closed her eyes and didn't answer. She didn't believe me anymore, which was a bad, bad feeling.

CHAPTER 23

fretted about the shelter-friends all night. In the morning, Walter took us for a walk in the neighborhood before he went to work. He put a leash on me. Any idea how humiliating that was? A leash! Koda? Sure. Ozzie, maybe. But me? Just no. I tried to hide behind him when we passed Jimmy standing outside his house drinking his coffee. He raised his cup to Walter.

"Morning, Walter!"

We got as far as the bend before Lilah's house and I refused to go any farther. I would not let her see me restrained by a leash. Ever. No matter how hard Walter tugged, I wouldn't budge. Finally, we turned back and went home.

All day I waited by the living room window, watching for Toby and Beth. All day, Ozzie kept after me to play.

C'mon! I gots toys outside.

After he bothered me a hundred bazillion times, I snarled at him.

Stop!

Ozzie being Ozzie, he snuck out through the tunnel under the garage wall, slipped through the weak spot in the fence, and came around to the front step and bounced up and down where I couldn't help but see him.

I gots out again!

He was still there, staring at me in the window, when Beth and Toby finally came. But something was wrong. They smelled of Leroi and Hickory and Quinn and Holly and Squirt and Hero and all the others. And they smelled of Huck. They'd already been to the shelter, which meant I wasn't going, which meant I didn't know if Huck had called for the white-truck man to come and take anyone away. This did not make me happy at all.

"Come on, guys," Beth said. She sounded cheerful, which was sort of reassuring, but still. "We're going to hike up the butte!"

We'd go past Lilah's house! I forgot about the shelter-friends for a while and gave myself a quick tongue grooming in all the places I could reach. Ozzie fell onto his front paws, put his hind end in the air, and wagged his thin little tail faster than the windshield wipers went in MomDoc's car on the rainiest of days.

Butte! Butte! C'mon, Di!

One more quick tidying up and I followed them all out the door. This time when we got close to Lilah's, I ran ahead around the bend and stopped in front of her house. Mr. Crandle wasn't on the porch swing. The curtains were pulled closed in the windows, and a car that wasn't his was in the driveway. I was just about to turn away when I saw Lilah's shiny black muzzle push the curtains aside and there she was, watching me watch for her. My heart got all fluttery and soft, and I would have melted right into the sidewalk if someone hadn't come and pulled my beloved away.

Toby and Beth and Ozzie caught up and called for me to follow.

"He's so cute about Lilah. I think he has a crush on her," Beth said.

"Maybe," Toby said. Then he walked a little faster so Beth couldn't see his face get flushed.

Nothing much happened while I waited for them at the base of the butte. Nothing except that Domino decided to follow us and woke me from a nap by stalking me through the tall grass like I was a mouse. He sprang onto my back, dug his paws in once really good, and sprinted away.

No sleepin' on the job, dude!

On the way back, Daisy, Jaws, and Luther met us in the

middle of the path before we got to Lilah's house. Daisy's tutu rash looked nearly all better. She came right up to me and sniffed my face.

Did you hear?

Hear what?

Mr. Crandle is gone.

Gone?

They just took him away!

Where? Where'd he go?

Hospital for sick people.

The last time Mr. Crandle had gone to the hospital, they'd called the shelter to pick Lilah up. I bolted away from the group and ran as fast as my three legs would take me all the way to her house, barking. I had to save her!

Lilah! Lilah!

The front gate was propped open. I careened around the corner and ran through, raced up onto the porch, and jumped against the door, barking as loud as I have ever barked before.

Lilah! Let me in!

No one came. If Mr. Cradle were home, he would have for sure. I braced my paws on the windowsill to see inside, but the curtains were shut tight.

Lilah!

Behind me, the stranger's car started up. I spun around and ran to the sidewalk but it was already moving slowly away. Two strangers were in the front seats, a man and a lady. I'd never seen either of them before. In the back, watching me out the window, was Lilah.

MahDi!

Lilah! Wait!

I barked, then exploded and sprinted down the road to chase after her.

Lilah!

Toby yelled for me to come back, but I couldn't stop. I had to save her. She watched me out the back window and pawed on the glass, barking for me, once, twice, three times. I struggled to catch up, barreling down the middle of the road, but the car was too fast. It stopped at the stop sign, then turned and drove out of sight.

Lilah was gone.

By dusk all the 'hood dogs knew that someone had kidnapped Lilah and they'd gathered in our front yard to watch the street in case the strange car brought her home. Daisy, Jaws, and Luther had followed us from the butte and stayed because their family was out and didn't know they had escaped from the yard. Pilot jumped her fence and joined the others. Peabody sniffed all up and down the road and sidewalk, searching for clues that might tell him where they'd taken her. Even with his super-duper-hyper-sniffer, he lost the scent at the stop sign.

Walter came later with Koda and laughed when he saw

all of them lined up in the front yard. As soon as Koda found out about Lilah, he came to me and sat quietly at the foot of the sofa.

Sorry 'bout ur fren. I'm here fur you.

There wasn't much any of us could do. We were just a bunch of rescued canines with no phones, no googles, no pockets, and no MomDoc. I turned away and kept watch out the window. Cars came and went, but none of them looked like the strange one that had taken her away.

Sometime in the night, when Walter was asleep and no cars had driven by for a very long time, I got up from the sofa, pushed my way through the doggie door to the garage, and snuck out through Ozzie's secret tunnel. The loose fence board squeaked when I nosed it aside, which is harder for a dog without The Spare to do easily because of balance. But once through, I galloped off in the dark, running across the neighbors' yards all the way to the yellow house at the end of the road.

The driveway was empty. The front gate was still open and the windows all dark. I propped my front paws on the sill again and tried to see through, but there was nothing. She was really gone. I spent the rest of the night wide awake on the back of the sofa, my ears perked toward the road, hoping for the sound of a strange car bringing her home. It never came.

CHAPTER 24

MomDoc called Walter first thing in the morning. We could hear the tone of her voice through the phone and it didn't sound cheerful at all. As soon as Walter hung up with her, he called Toby.

"I'm going to have to go help her," he said. "All kinds of complications and the move is bigger than she expected. She was wondering if your dad would let you stay here tonight and part of tomorrow?"

He paced around the kitchen with the phone to his ear, nodding, then talking, then nodding again.

"Thank you, Toby," he said. "I'll leave a note about Koda's food on the counter. We'll stay in touch."

Beth and Toby didn't come for us until the afternoon. By that time I was in such a state about Lilah and things happening at the shelter that my belly wasn't cooperating one bit. I snapped at Ozzie and Koda.

"Poor Koda," Beth said. She wrapped her arms around his neck. "Sorry you have to stay here, but we'll get you a doggie cone on the way back."

Finally, Beth tucked me into the wicker basket and we were off. I curled up deep inside and let the motion of cruising down the road put me to sleep. It had been a very long night.

Trouble was already brewing when we got to the shelter. Huck was stomping around the office grumbling and told Toby that Ozzie and I couldn't go back into the kennel room.

"They get them all riled up and then I'm stuck here until they calm down."

"They'll be fine, Huck, I promise," Toby said.

Huck's face swelled up again and it made his eyes look like two tiny dots on a pink balloon.

"I said no!"

Beth pulled Ozzie closer in her arms. "How about if Toby and I clean *all* the kennels *and* the play yard and get them all out for exercise and do the water by ourselves. All of it. Can they come with us then?"

Huck picked at a fingernail and watched me waiting by the door to the kennel room. "You'd better do a good job, that's all I gotta say," he said. "And keep them quiet. I got a head-ache. Only a few more days and I'm out."

Beth and Toby looked at each other quickly.

"Who's coming then?" Toby asked.

Huck stuck a toothpick into his mouth and chewed. "They tell me Mike's coming back. I'll believe it when I see the whites of his eyes comin' through the door."

I didn't like the way he sneered at them, but I knew better than to do anything about it. I pawed at the door.

"Go on then, get to work," he said, flipping his hand in the air. "Oh yeah and that dog who was in quarantine? He's in the regular room now. Don't move him back."

"Hickory?"

"Yeah, whatever. Don't move him! I'm tired of walkin' back and forth through this place all day. One dog here, a cat there, a whole mess in that noisy room and then them others scattered all willy-nilly. I'm sick of it. Someone tried to make me come back after I left last night to take a dog, but I said no. They're bringing some mutt today and that's it!" He slammed the mitt on the desk. "Now get outta here, go to work!"

We all rushed into the kennel room. Leroi came to her gate as soon as she saw us.

You're back.

Toby moved quickly down the aisle and found Hickory

near the end. Beth looked around until she saw Holly on the other side, standing at her gate, wagging her tail.

"Holly!"

Quinn was still next to Leroi, lying on her cushion with Stuffy tucked under her chin. She raised her head.

Marilease?

Still waiting. Always waiting. Hopefully, MomDoc would be able to find Marilease once she got back.

Soon.

Hickory trotted out of his kennel with barely any sign of a limp. Toby kneeled and ruffled his fur, smiling.

"He looks okay. I guess it was time to move him out here."

"That means he's up for adoption now, doesn't it?" Beth asked.

Toby's eyes shadowed over, but he smiled through it and rubbed his hand along Hickory's back. "Yeah, I guess it does. I hope he gets just the right home. Anyway, let's take him out and see how he does."

They let Hickory out with just me and Ozzie at first. He was quick to let Ozzie know he wasn't a run-and-play kind of guy, so Beth threw the ball over and over again to keep Ozzie happy. Hickory meandered around, sniffing the fence line, relieving himself on the back side of the yard by the lone tree, then he went to where Toby was sitting, scratched out a well in the dirt, and curled up.

Beth brought out Leroi and Quinn next.

"Good choice, the older ones go together with Hickory because he still needs quiet," Toby said.

He was sitting on the ground, his back against the fence, with Hickory in his little well beside him. Leroi and Quinn did their business then went to the other part of the fence and sat side by side to watch down the road. Stuffy lay on the ground between them. Ozzie bounded over with a tennis ball in his mouth, dropped it beside Leroi, and spun around, his eyes bright and his tail wagging.

Play?

I called him away.

No play, they're waiting.

"Hey, Ozzie, look what I found!"

Beth held up a stuffed squirrel toy, the one Ozzie had buried behind the building some time back. He raced over to her and jumped into the air, trying to get it from her hands, but his little mini-pistons couldn't propel him off the ground high enough, so Beth tossed it across the grass away from Leroi and Quinn.

The dogs came out in groups and Toby and Beth took turns staying with them or going inside to do cleaning. Squirt went out with Bear and Holly and the three of them wore Ozzie out. The last group included Hero and the tiny papillon. Everywhere the little dog with the butterfly ears went, Hero followed, watching, guarding her. When they rested, the papillon curled up against his belly.

I take good care of her.

Toby and Beth had gone inside to see to the cats in the cat room. I was dozing in the shade, still fretting about Lilah, when a car door slammed in the parking lot on the other side of the building. A few minutes later, there was a familiar bark and a frightened yelp coming from inside the kennel room. I knew that bark.

I knew that bark!

The door to the play yard was still propped open. I made a run for it.

Let me forewarn you, what I saw should never happen. I am sorry I have to share this, but it's important you understand why I went after Huck, and why we were all kicked out of the shelter that afternoon.

I raced around the corner, through the door, and into the back of the room, and there she was. My beautiful Lilah, cowering in the back of a kennel. Huck was hanging an orange tag on the front of the gate.

"I'm in charge here, dog, and you're one too many for me. I'm done. You're outta here first thing Monday."

Then he sliced his finger across his throat.

Lilah!

She looked at me with her tail tucked, her head down, her

eyes up, and every part of her body shaking.

Help me. . . .

A growl trembled in my throat. Huck saw me and smacked the mitt against his other hand, sneering.

"Don't give me that, Lame-O. I worked my buns off clearing dogs outta here and now someone dumps another one on me? No siree, mister. I've been overrun for too long, and your little lady-vet ain't around to tell me how to do my job anymore."

He held up a stack of the orange tags and laughed, his eyes glistening and dark.

"Listen to me, talking to you like you get it. I must have tipped over the edge of crazy from being here so long."

Ozzie heard the same yelp I did and sprinted down the aisle toward us. Just as he got close, the look in Huck's face changed to both rage and fear.

"Stay away, you little creep!"

He swung his leg out and plowed the toe of his boot into Ozzie's side, shoving him away. Ozzie landed, stunned, on the concrete. And you know what Huck did? He laughed. Out loud.

"I told you to keep away, you little mutts!"

That's when I went after him. I'm sure you understand. My teeth hit flesh and I tasted blood. Huck screamed and swung his foot at me but hit the kennel wall instead. I spun away and slid across the floor. Sweat dripped off his nose. He wiped his mouth with the back of his hand then spit onto the floor.

"Where's that kid?" he screamed.

I scrambled up and rushed to Lilah's gate, every hair, every bit of flesh, everything in my body on fire.

Lilah!

MahDi!

Toby ran in from the cat room carrying a broom and dustpan. Beth was right behind him with a bag of cat food in her arms. They both slammed to a stop about halfway to us.

"What happened?" Toby asked, his voice shaking. He dropped the broom and dustpan to the floor.

"Get these beasts out of here. Now!" Huck said, breathing heavily. "Both of 'em tried to bite me. Look at my leg!"

His pants were stained with a dark spot just the tiniest bit on the back of his calf, but who's to say that stain wasn't already there? Ozzie sat up in the middle of the aisle, dazed and confused. Bits of blood clung to the curly hair around his mouth. For the first time I saw how Beth looked like Lydia. Curls of hair sprang in tight bunches around her face, and she had that same look of fury. She let go of the cat food bag and went to Ozzie.

Toby squeezed his hands into tight balls. "What did you do to him?"

"Moved him out of the way with my boot, just like this one." He laughed again and pointed to Lilah's kennel gate. "They didn't like me puttin' on the orange tag."

"Why are you doing that?" Toby asked. "You said you're out of here next week, what do you care if there's an extra dog?"

Huck pulled a folded paper from his back pocket and held it open.

"Says right here, acting manager's discretion." He poked himself in the chest. "That's me, acting manager. My discretion. Or is that too big a word for you, slowpoke?"

Lilah crept closer to me and lowered her head.

Help?

I sniffed her through the chain links.

I'm here.

Toby took a couple steps toward us, not getting too close to Huck but able to see inside the kennel. "Is that Lilah?"

"I don't know what her name is, but those people said keeping it was a hardship on their old, sick pops. Told me to get rid of her, so now she's here, and there ain't nothing you can do about it."

Toby didn't hesitate this time, he went to the gate and twisted the orange tag until it broke off, then turned to face Huck.

"I don't know who the people were that brought her, but

this dog has a home, she's my neighbor."

"Well, bully for her, she was turned in. And besides, I don't answer to you, kid. Get out of here."

Beth was fired up like I'd never seen her before. "She's microchipped! You can see who she belongs to!"

"Too bad I can't read that micro-whatever machine, it's probably broken."

Toby reached for the handle on Lilah's gate. Huck clamped his pudgy pale hand over Toby's big dark one and forced it away.

"Just let us take her, Huck, then we'll be out of your way," Toby said quietly.

Down the aisle I heard Leroi whining and someone else pawing at their gate.

Huck held out his hand. "Gimme that tag."

Toby stuffed the orange tag back into his pocket. "No, I'm taking her with me."

"I told you, that dog ain't going nowhere, unless you can prove who her owner is. Then I gotta go through all the paperwork stuff and you have to pay the eighty bucks."

Toby pulled out his wallet and shuffled through some paper money.

"I have thirty-eight."

"It's eighty. Besides, computer's shut down for the day and I've got dinner and a beer waiting."

Toby balled his fists tight. Beth stepped in between him and Huck.

"Come on, Toby, we'll get the money and come back in the morning," she said so quietly I almost couldn't hear. Toby didn't move, he didn't take his eyes off Huck.

"Gimme the tag and get out of here," Huck said.

Toby shook his head. "No tag."

Huck flicked his hand. "Whatever. I got plenty of 'em."

Lilah pressed her body against the gate. A tuft of shiny black hair poked through, and two velvety brown eyes pleaded with me to free her. Just seeing her trapped and frightened like that sent me into a rage of my own. I couldn't help it, I jumped up high behind Huck and ripped a chunk from the back of his britches. He screamed like someone was hauling him off to slaughter, turned, and swung his boot at me again, but he missed, so he slammed his fist against the gate instead. The crazed, wild look was back. He jumped toward Toby, screaming.

"Get out, all of you, now!"

Lilah jerked away, tumbled backward to the corner, and cowered against the wall.

What's happening?

Huck made a fist and put it in front of Toby's face. "I said get out!"

"Come on," Beth said. "Let's go."

Toby had to lift me up to get me to leave. I wriggled in his arms and watched over his shoulder as Lilah got smaller and farther away. I can't explain what it felt like to go past all the faces of the shelter-friends, every one of them begging for help. None of them wanted to be left behind. Quinn stood at her gate with Stuffy in her mouth. Leroi pawed and pleaded.

Don't leave us here!

There was nothing I could do. I whined and barked but Toby kept walking, so finally I buried my face in his shoulder and closed my eyes.

CHAPTER 25

I didn't eat. I couldn't sleep. I went from the back of the sofa to the kitchen to the backyard to the sofa again all evening. Toby called MomDoc and told her what had happened, and he said he was going to get Lilah the next day, but it wasn't good enough. What if Huck got there early? What if the white-truck man made a special trip before we got there? What if what if what if?

Long after dark, I climbed down from the sofa and moved to my kitchen bed, circled, scratched, circled again, and lay down. I couldn't be still. Lilah was in danger. I had to save her. But how? Ozzie was sleeping upstairs with Toby and Koda. Patches of white bobbed in the darkness. Domino slunk up beside me and stretched.

What are you so worked up about?

Lilah's in trouble.

He sat on his haunches and licked his paws.

What are you going to do about it?

What was I going to do? What could I do? What must I do?
I jumped up from the bed.

I'm going to save her.

The old cat stretched and arched his back, then disappeared. A minute later I heard a padding, *tap-tap-tap*, on the
stairs. Ozzie!

Di?

I'm going to save her.

I stood there for a second as if the answer to how might
suddenly come to me, but it didn't. Nothing except that I
knew I had to act. I had to go. Ozzie didn't blink. He didn't
hesitate.

K, Di. I'll go, too.

He trotted past me with sleep still in his eyes.

Let's go, fren.

We were headed toward the laundry room doggie door
when Koda appeared at the top of the stairs.

Can I go?

He wanted to help save Lilah, but if suddenly there were
no dogs on the bed beside Toby, he might wake up and stop
us. I stepped to the bottom of the stairs and looked up.

Your job is to stay with Toby so he doesn't wake up and find out we're gone.

Koda wagged his tail.

Good job?

Yes, very important.

K. I do good job.

Then he turned and went back down the hall to the bed where Toby was sleeping.

Domino followed and we left the house the same way we had before, through the tunnel under the garage wall and the loose fence board on the side of the yard. The three of us ran down the middle of the street in the night. We passed Jimmy's house, then Daisy, Jaws, and Luther's. Pilot's house was next, then Peabody's and finally Lilah's. They were all as dark as Lilah's coat. It was deep in the night, no longer the evening before, but still far from morning. All dogs and their families would be cozy in their beds, fast asleep.

We turned off the path and ran across the field at Toby's school. If anyone had seen us—a raggedy terrier still sore from being kicked, a three-legged canine the size, shape, and color of a red fox, and a black-and-white, one-eyed, toothless, tailless cat who might be confused for a skunk in the dark— well, just imagine.

We skirted the edge of the houses, steering clear of the beams from any lights. One street, then another, and another until we went through the patch of woods and climbed the hill to the road where the tire had blown out beside me. I didn't stop this time. I didn't care if a car was coming, Lilah was in danger. I bolted across the road with Ozzie and Domino trailing and came up on the back side of the shelter. Streetlamps spilled light around the edge of the fenced play yard. I could climb that fence, I knew how, but then what? The door to the kennel room was shut. How would we get inside? I paced along the edge, thinking, trying to solve the puzzle. Domino scaled the fence easily, dropped to the other side, and disappeared.

Ozzie trotted up and down, sniffing, then scratching, then sniffing again.

How we get her out?

I'm thinking.

I have an idea!

Before I could say anything, he turned, revved up his mini-pistons, and bolted across the road into the night. He was gone.

Domino stalked along the bottom of the fence on the other side.

Great. Now it's just you and me.

I was wound up tighter than I'd ever been before. I ran around to the far side of the building and stood outside the private run to that last kennel on the right. The one where Lilah was waiting for me. I barked softly and she scratched at the door leading to her yard.

It's me.

She whined, then stood up on her hind feet, and I could just see the top of her head over the sliver of window glass.

Lilah! I'm here!

Domino had gone off somewhere again. I was all alone. I trotted around the entire shelter building, past the front porch, along the side where the private runs were, and to the back again where Ozzie and I had been before. I couldn't just wait for daylight when Huck showed up. I couldn't just wait for Toby to wake up and see me missing. I wasn't going to wait long enough for the white truck to pull into the driveway. I had to do something. I had to save her.

Digging holes is another thing that is harder without The Spare, but I started on one, anyway. If I dug at the base of that fence long enough I'd at least be able to get into the play yard and maybe I could figure something else out then. I had to take more breaks than a younger dog would, and more than a dog with four legs who could balance better while digging, but I kept at it until I had scraped out enough to get my head under the fence.

A noise was coming from the woods across the road. Leaves rustling, a grunt, a murmur. Slowly, a large mass topped the hill and started to cross out of the dark and into the light. Ozzie, Daisy, Jaws and Luther, Pilot and Peabody. Daisy stepped up next to Ozzie.

We're here to help.

Behind them, Peabody's nose was to the ground. He trotted faster than I'd ever seen him move, back and forth through the grass, then around the side of the shelter. He stopped by Lilah's backyard.

I detect her in there.

Daisy checked the place where I'd started digging a hole.

Jaws! Luther! Ozzie! Dig! Right here. Big enough to get Lilah through.

Her henchmen dropped their heads and started shoveling dirt with their front paws so fast it flew out behind them.

Peabody, Pilot, keep circling the building.

What do we do?

Sniff out trouble coming. Pilot, you alert us at once. I'll watch the road. Go!

Ozzie started scratching at the ground beside Jaws. Peabody and Pilot circled twice before there was a hole big enough for me to slip under. I scrambled under and pushed through with Ozzie right behind me. We were in. Jaws's and Luther's paws worked furiously, scratching, digging, dirt flying, to get the hole big enough for Lilah, but it didn't matter. We were stuck. The door into the kennel room was shut. I ran back and forth, scratched and whined and stopped beside Ozzie outside the door.

Wut we do now?

We will find a way in!

We heard a hiss from overhead and looked up to see

Domino creeping along the doorframe.

Hiss. Get back!

He sank onto his haunches, his body pressed against the wall with barely enough room to keep both paws on the ledge. With one swift plunge, he flew off, grabbed the safety rope midair, and gripped tight with all four paws.

Clear the decks! Man down!

It was just enough force. The door swung open just as Domino let go and dropped to the earth.

Daisy raced across the yard.

I'll hold the door! Get her out! Get her out!

Me and Ozzie and Domino hurtled through and skidded to a stop when we got inside. Light from the streetlamps cast an eerie glow through the windows, spilling yellow shadows across the faces of every dog, in every kennel, as they sat by their gates, silent, watching.

Not one of them moved. Not one of them jumped with joy and surprise to see us. Their eyes told the only story that mattered.

Because along with their sad faces, that light illuminated the bright orange tags hanging from

every

single

gate.

My body shook. Ozzie turned a full circle, looking at all the kennels with all the orange tags, and gave a tiny whimper.

Domino arched his back, hissed, and disappeared. I was pulled to action by the scent of coconut shampoo and went straight to Lilah.

I knew you'd come.

Daisy was still holding the door when Jaws and Luther, Pilot and Peabody stepped inside the room.

Wut the heck?

Daisy was looking at Hero in his kennel and barked orders to the others.

See that big white dog? He'll need a much bigger hole to get out of here. Back outside, now!

All up and down the aisle the shelter-friends watched and waited. Holly sat upright in front of her gate, her coat shimmering in the odd light.

Help me?

Hickory was standing strong on his four legs now, as if he'd never injured one. Quinn paced nervously from one end of her kennel to the other with Stuffy clenched in her jaw. Squirt trembled so hard her curls jiggled. She was pressed against the wall between her kennel and Bear's. He was on the other side, pressing just as hard so their bodies touched through the chain links.

He took Monkey away.

Hero stood at his gate, his tail curled tight over his back, the hairs on the scruff around his neck raised and thick.

I don' wanna be useless!

Next to him the little black-and-white papillon pulled her blanket off her bed, dragged it across the floor, and wrapped herself inside. All I could see were her butterfly ears and her eyes.

Ozzie sat beside me.

Now wut?

Now what? Now what?

First, we get them out.

I went to Lilah's kennel and tucked one paw into a chain link, grabbed the next one, hopped off my back leg, and stuck that paw into a lower link, then inched my way up until my nose reached the latch on her gate.

This!

This was why I learned to climb a fence so many years ago. It was for this moment—the one when I would save Lilah. I held tight and pushed hard at the lever with my nose, but it didn't flip. The orange tag was jammed in between the lock and the gate so it wouldn't open. Lilah whimpered. I let myself drop to the floor.

Don't worry. I'm just resting.

Outside, Jaws and Luther were digging a bigger hole so we could get Hero out with everyone else. Pilot and Peabody were doing their part keeping watch, ready to sound the alarm if someone came, although if you'd asked, not one of us would have been able to tell you what we'd do. Daisy was still blocking the door with her stout little body. Ozzie sprinted up and down the aisle, stopping at each kennel, jumping up and knocking the orange tags off. Nine pairs of eyes watched us. Nine souls trusted us. Nine dogs needed to be saved.

I climbed Lilah's gate again and this time I got the orange tag in my teeth, clenched my jaw, and dropped to the floor, pulling the tag with me. I was getting ready to jump and flip the latch to open her gate when Domino leaped up, holding himself tight to the gate with three paws stuffed through the chain links. With the fourth paw, he flipped the lever. We heard a *clack* sound. Lilah's gate swung open with Domino still attached. She was free.

I licked her face and she batted those long lashes at me, but I still had work to do.

Domino, you take this side, I'll go over there!

One by one, Domino and I climbed up the chain link of every kennel and opened the gates. Daisy barked orders.

Let's go, let's go, out to the yard, wait for instructions! Be quiet!

The shelter-friends all ran out with me and Ozzie. Pilot herded them into a tight group, and Daisy stayed at the door waiting for Peabody, who was sniffing out each kennel to be sure no one was left behind, to give the all clear. Bear yelped and broke away from the pack, ran across the yard, and vanished around the dark side of the building. When he came back he had two toys in his mouth—his one-armed Monkey and a rubber squeaky mouse he laid at the papillon's paws.

Leroi looked at me, worried.

Now what?

It was the look in her eyes that made what happened next perfectly clear. I knew exactly what to do. I didn't have just Lilah to save anymore, I had a group of shelter-friends who needed homes, and a bunch of homes that needed their love. My heart lifted in a way that is hard to explain without knowing all the words, but there was a mixture of relief and joy and maybe a hint of redemption.

I might not have saved those dogs from my life before MomDoc, but these ones here, they would all be just fine.

Let's go. Let's go fill some lives.

CHAPTER 26

Story's family lived the farthest away from the shelter, so we went there first. It was the place where, after a rough start in life, a big furry dog had been so happy, carrying children around on his back. It was the place where his family was still grieving. The road leading to the house was long, sandy, and dark, and we left dust swirling behind us like a mini-tornado. When we got close, everyone stood silently, waiting for orders.

Hero!

He trotted up beside me.

This family needs you.

He looked at the house. The front porch light was on,

bright and welcoming. Story's outside bed was still beside the door.

Wut do I do here?

See that big bed? It belonged to one of the finest dogs I've ever known. You lie on that bed and wait. They'll find you in the morning.

He dipped his head.

I won't be useless anymore?

Here you are needed exactly as you are.

His tail wagged all the way up the steps, and when he climbed onto the bed and circled, he lay down and looked up at us once more to say goodbye.

We were about halfway up that long road when Leroi trotted up next to me.

Do you know where Murph lives?

No. But Mike is home now. You'll go there.

Peabody pushed through the crowd of dogs and Domino.

My super-duper-hyper-sniffer detected his scent a ways back. I'll take her.

Leroi licked my ear and nuzzled my neck.

Thank you, friend. I'll never forget.

She and Peabody trotted off into the night, Peabody's nose flush to the ground, Leroi's head up and eyes alert, watching for familiar signs from the many times Mike had taken her home.

We went off the other way, toward Fred the boxer's house. His human had told MomDoc the last time Fred got quilled by the porcupine that he needed a friend to play with to keep him out of trouble. Bear would be perfect. They'd make a great team. I took Bear around to the back door.

Fred the boxer needs you.

Bear lowered his head, sniffed, then lay down with the one-armed monkey by his side.

I smell a new friend right here.

We were all tiring out, but whenever someone lagged behind, Pilot nipped and pushed them forward. Ozzie came up beside me.

Who's next?

The lady next door to Mrs. Comfort who comes over to pat Tootsie.

She wanna dog?

She does now.

When we got to the house, I called to the papillon, Penelope. She stared at the fancy scrollwork in the wood above the porch. She gawked at the immaculate white picket fence surrounding a garden full of roses, and the small tree with fancy bird feeders hanging from the branches.

It's so beautiful!

A home for you.

She wants me?

She will love you.

Penelope squeezed through the fence, bounced up the walkway, and climbed into a wooden tub of flowers by the door and nestled in to wait. All we could see were her butterfly ears poking out of the potted geraniums.

Ozzie laid his chin on my back.

You k, Di?

My old body ached, but my heart felt happy and new.

I'm okay. You okay?

He nudged my ear.

So happy.

Lucy's house was the last one before our street. We went there next. The orange goldfish balloon still floated above the fence, just like it had a few days before.

Squirt!

She came forward and I led her to the front porch next to a basket of yellow chrysanthemums.

I stay here?

Yes. Lucy has wanted a dog for a very long time.

I didn't tell her about the allergies, or that the mom was afraid to have a dog. Somehow, though, I had faith that whoever found Squirt the next morning, they'd know right away it was meant to be.

Squirt curled up next to the basket.

I can't wait to see her.

Lucy's house was near Toby's school, so we took the short-cut on the path that went by Lilah's house.

You'll come with me until Mr. Crandle is home.

Lilah wagged her tail, but when we got to the yellow house, the porch light was on. Lilah stopped abruptly, head high, tail up over her back, her eyes on the figure moving back and forth on the swing. Mr. Crandle was wrapped in a blanket, his face whiter than I'd ever seen, and he was gently pushing against the floor with his toe. Lilah quivered, ready to rush to him, but the door opened and a lady stepped out.

"Mr. Crandle, please come inside and try to sleep a little. We'll find where they took her tomorrow, I promise."

Are those the people that took you away?

Lilah studied the lady for a second.

No.

Her tail swung from side to side and she lowered her chest to the ground. Then, with a burst of joy and energy, she bounded out of the shadows and ran to the front gate, barking and springing off the ground. The lady moved quickly down the walkway to let her in. Lilah didn't even look back. She raced up the steps to Mr. Crandle and stopped in front of him, resting her head very gently on his lap.

"Oh, my beautiful girl, it is a dream come true. You have appeared before me as the stars pop into the sky. I was so worried when you weren't here, but now you've come home."

Yes, home.

The night had worn on me and the fringes of daylight were starting to lighten the sky. Lilah was safe. I would see her another time. Right then, we still had work to do. I turned away.

Let's go.

Somewhere between Mr. Crandle's and Jimmy's houses, Pilot peeled away and disappeared to go home. She'd done good work. Domino's work was done, and he went ahead of us, too. The rest of us stopped beside Jimmy's mailbox. Quinn was still waiting for Marilease the same way Jimmy was waiting for Bullseye. It was the perfect match.

You are needed here.

Quinn didn't hesitate. She knew exactly where she was meant to be. We watched from the last of the night's shadows as the old girl trotted happily up the walkway with Stuffy in her mouth, no sign of a limp. Jimmy opened his front door wearing a ragged bathrobe, his hair standing on end, and a coffee cup in one hand. He stooped down to pick up his newspaper right as Quinn trotted past. She wasn't waiting for an invitation to cross over the threshold into her new home.

Jimmy searched the street for a sign of who might have brought her to him, but Holly, Hickory, Ozzie, and I were on the other side of the road in the shadows. He shook his head and raised his coffee cup to the sky.

"Okay, Universe, I hear you loud and clear."

Then he turned and followed his dog inside.

Holly sniffed out Beth's house next door to ours. She didn't need anyone to show her where she belonged, whether Lydia thought they were ready or not.

Beth! Beth!

She bounded across the yard, jumped over a toy truck, climbed onto the porch swing, and curled up to wait for the new day.

Thank you, MahDi.

Hickory came up beside me looking worried. He'd started limping a while back, but he hadn't complained once.

Can I go with Toby?

Yes, as it should be.

Toby and Koda were still sleeping upstairs when me and Ozzie and Hickory pushed through the loose fence board behind our house. Hickory couldn't fit into the tunnel to get inside the garage, so we went around to the glass kitchen door and pushed, hoping it wasn't latched. No such luck.

You'll have to wait here.

Hickory lapped up the water from the bowl on the deck, then climbed onto one of the chairs, scratched, circled, and lay down.

I'm happier outside. You go in.

Then he tucked his face into the curve of his body to sleep.

With the last bit of energy we had, Ozzie and I pushed through the tunnel into the garage and the laundry room doggie door, drank the entire bowl of water in the kitchen, then lay down on our beds, curled up together, and fell fast asleep.

Nine souls had been saved that night. And nine families were now complete.

CHAPTER 27

One Month Later

The room at Toby and Beth's school where Lydia let us hold the free spay-and-neuter clinic and adoption day all in one smelled like stinky shoes and sweat and that stuff they use to clean the floors at the clinic. At least when we first got there it did. Afterward it smelled of a hundred dogs and cats who had come in and out through the day.

As soon as the surgery tables were draped in blue sheets and shiny bins with the tools MomDoc and the other two vets would use were set out, and the recovery area was ready with cushy beds and water and toys, and a table with all kinds of papers and writing things was set up front by the door, the first of one hundred dogs scheduled came in, and I went to work.

He was a young Saint Bernard mix with paws that promised he'd at least double in size by the time he was grown, with large droopy eyes and a classic bit of drool trickling from the corner of his mouth.

Hey, Bernie, here for the snip-snip?

He leaned his body against the leg of the boy holding his leash and looked at me suspiciously.

How'd u know my name?

Lucky guess.

Where'd ur leg go?

Was just a spare. Didn't need it.

To prove it, I trotted a few steps away, then did a handstand and walked to him, landing slightly off-balance on all three legs. Beth, who was sitting at the check-in desk with Lydia, laughed, then tossed me a cookie. I picked it up off the floor before Bernie could steal it. Dogs getting the snip-snip can't eat before they go to sleep.

See? Things come off and life is better. You'll get treats after you wake up.

Bernie raised his head and wagged his tail.

For reals?

For reals.

Mike and Rebecca and Toby set up everything for the adoption part of the day on the other side of the gymnasium. There was a round area bordered by a low fence where people could take their time finding just the right dog, plus a mop and bucket of water for cleanup of the inevitable accidents, balls and rope toys, and cushions for sitting.

"I think we're ready for the dogs," Mike said when it was all done.

"I'll get them," Toby said. "Beth's going to help."

They brought them in one at a time and Rebecca checked each off her list. Some of the dogs to be adopted had come into our shelter after the midnight rescue. But there were still too many dogs in other shelters, so some of them had come from farther away. I went to them first.

A baby beagle-Lab mix with brown eyes and a pink bow tied around her neck came in first. Beth set her crate down.

"It says her name is Lily, eight months old," she told Rebecca.

Rebecca nodded. "Lily, got it. One down, twenty-three to go."

Lily tapped a white-tipped paw against the gate.

Hello, excuse me, can you tell me where I am?

We sniffed noses. Lily was friendly, non-alpha, and would do great with kids.

You're here to find a new home.

I didn't mind my old one, can't I go back?

I never knew how to answer those kinds of questions, so I said what usually seemed right.

There's a better family looking for you. Don't worry.

Toby carried in a crate with a cattle dog who looked like

he could have been Quinn's brother. "Name is Cutter, male, heeler," he told Rebecca. "Six years old."

Rebecca leaned down to peek at Cutter. "He's cute. He'll need an active home."

Cutter looked uncomfortable, like he'd spent too much time in a crate. I went over and he stood to greet me.

New home again?

Looks like it, buddy.

Cutter sat down.

Can I go someplace where they'll give me work?

You get bored?

There's lots of stuff to chew, but none of them like that.

Don't worry. Mike will find just the right home.

Cool.

By lunchtime, the wall was lined with crates full of assorted terriers and poodles, a husky, a couple of Lab-types, and a litter of little black, white, and brown pups who reminded me of my brothers and sisters from so long ago. There were long-haired dogs, short-haired dogs, young dogs, senior dogs, and one that was every bit as big as Moose. But the last one that came in broke my heart. She was tan and white with a crooked neck, a pink snub nose, and tiny scratch marks all across her swollen belly. She had just been pulled away from a litter of puppies. Everything about her smelled sad and lonely.

"This is Luna," Toby said. "Staffordshire terrier, three years old, neck is crooked from an accident." He kneeled in front of her and put his hand on the door of the crate. "She's super quiet but she doesn't look up. She just stares at the floor all the time. I think she misses her puppies."

Rebecca's face fell when she saw Luna. "Poor thing, probably dumped by a puppy mill. So awful."

She sat down on the floor in front of Luna's crate and pushed a tiny treat through the door. It landed on the floor. Luna just stared.

"You know what, Luna?" Rebecca said. "We're going to send you home today with people who will cherish you and love you just the way you are."

A little later I was up front helping Beth and Lydia check in the dogs and cats coming for the snip-snip when Jimmy ran in with Quinn by his side and a cardboard box in his hands.

"Where's Doc?" he asked.

Lydia pointed toward the back of the room. "But you shouldn't go there with another dog, they're doing surgeries."

"She's gotta come with me. It's important," he said. "Come on, girl!"

I followed behind them, past the crates where dogs were waiting to be adopted. Luna was in the last one, staring at the pile of uneaten treats on the floor. I'd come back to her. First, I had to find out what was up with Jimmy.

"Doc! Doc!" Jimmy called. "I met her! I met that lady and look what she brung me!"

MomDoc looked up from a sleeping sheltie who was laid out on its back on the table. Its belly was already shaved.

"What lady?"

"Marilease, the one who used to have Quinn!"

He set the box down on a table and opened the lid.

"My girl was a champion dog," he said. "And the lady wanted me to have this!"

He lifted a tall gold-colored statue on a wooden base and held it up for MomDoc to see.

"Jimmy, that's amazing," she said. "Did she get to see Quinn?"

"Yeah, she did. I was scared she was gonna take her away, but she said no, that's why she signed them papers last month for me. She's gonna send me a picture, too, of Quinn doing all her tricks in a ring, and I'm gonna put it right up next to the picture of me getting gored by that bull when I was a rodeo clown."

MomDoc laughed, then picked up one of the shiny tools to start the snip-snip on the sheltie.

"I'm really glad, Jimmy. For all of you."

Ever since the night we'd taken Quinn to his house and she'd marched inside like she owned the place, Jimmy didn't go anywhere without her. He told anyone who would listen about the rescue miracle and what a brilliant dog she was. And when MomDoc told him that Marilease had agreed to let him keep her, he'd thrown a party. All the dogs from the 'hood played a game of Rodeo in the street and he'd sent everyone home with their own red handkerchief.

MomDoc knew what we'd done that night, but she didn't tell anyone. The next day when Huck found everyone gone, he walked out of the shelter and never came back. Mike said he'd been dismissed from the police force training and no one ever heard from him again. The newspaper wrote a bunch of stories about the dogs getting busted out instead of going off for The Unthinkable, and the first one was with a picture of Mike standing in the aisle of the empty kennel room the day he came back to work.

Things were just settling down in the gymnasium again when something upset Leroi. She yelped like she'd been stung by a bee and bolted out from under the adoption table, sprinting toward the front, howling.

"Loose dog!"

I ran after her, but by the time I caught up she was straddling a man on the floor, licking his face and making that noise all dogs who have been loved by a human understand. The noise that comes from the place we hold in our hearts forever. The man lifted his arms and wrapped them tight around Leroi's body.

"Leroi, my Leroi, you waited."

Murph.

He'd made it home after all.

A photographer came from the newspaper to take a picture at the end of the day. Most of the dogs we'd busted out of the shelter came, too, and the photographer almost left when he saw how many dogs and humans he had to fit into that one shot.

"No one told me to bring a wide-angle lens!"

"Wait," MomDoc said. "We can make it work. We'll get everyone on the bleachers."

Lucy came with her dad. She had her mask and gloves on, "Because of the other dogs, not Squirt," she said. Allison, who had been following the story and found out where Squirt had landed, sat on one side of Squirt with Lucy on the other.

Hero was so excited to show me his new family he dragged one of the kids halfway across the room.

See my people! They love me!

They love you just the way you are.

Mrs. Comfort brought Tootsie and her neighbor who carried Penelope in her purse.

"Tootsie wanted to show off her new nails and her new friend."

You happy?

Tootsie curled into Mrs. Comfort's lap.

Forever kind of happy.

Penelope's ears perked up, and I knew she'd found just the right home, too.

MomDoc, Auntie, and Walter sat on the lowest bench between me and Ozzie and Koda. Walter held up a picture of Bailey from a day at the lake when he was wearing his life jacket. "Bailey is the reason we met, and the reason Koda found his forever home."

Murph sat with Mike and Rebecca, his arm draped across Leroi's back. He was thin and wore old clothes and his skin was pale, but his smile was so big nothing else mattered. Mike told MomDoc that Murph was going to work at the shelter since Toby and Beth were back in school. "He's the kind of person we need, not the likes of Huck."

Rebecca held on to Luna's collar. That sweet, sad dog had finally looked up, and when she did, it was into Rebecca's eyes. I'd heard Rebecca say it myself. "Oh, she's coming home with us."

Jimmy held up Quinn's trophy and Beth sat cross-legged on the floor, front and center, with her arm looped under Holly's neck. Toby was behind her with Hickory snuggled up close, a little nervous, but willing to stay out of loyalty to his new boy. Bear was somewhere on the benches behind us.

Mr. Crandle came in last with a lady pushing his wheel-chair, Lilah's leash wrapped tight around his hand. Her newly washed coat fell in silky black waves and when she walked past me, the lovely smell of coconut and peppermints made my heart swing sideways. They got settled at the end of the bleachers and Lilah called to me.

MahDi, please come?

I looked up at MomDoc and she smiled. "Go on, I don't blame you one bit."

When everyone was finally in place, the photographer looked through his lens, moved back a few steps, then counted with his finger.

"This is bigger than any reunion I've ever done."

He raised the camera to his face.

"Wait! Where's Domino?" Auntie cried.

That old cat was never going to be left behind in something this important. He'd positioned himself high up on top of a cabinet at the end of the bleachers, waiting. When Auntie called his name he sank back on his haunches, then launched himself through the air and flew in front of everyone else, his legs stretched out to each side like a flying squirrel, with his toothless mouth open wide.

CLICK! CLICK!

CLICK! CLICK!

Monday, the clinic was hopping. This time, it was people bringing in the newspaper to show us the picture, like we hadn't already seen it.

As if . . .

"Look! You're famous, MahDi!"

"Hey, let me get my picture taken with MahDi, and where's Ozzie?"

All morning was like that. The good news was, I got tons of treats. Ozzie, too. Even Domino got to come with us for the day, but he wasn't impressed by all the commotion over his acrobatics; he just stretched out and slept.

I was near the window at the front door, sniffing a man's shoes, when a girl rode up outside on a bike with pink streamers flying off the handles. She leaned the bike against the building, then came inside slowly, almost like she was afraid. When she saw me watching her, she leaned down and patted the top of my head.

"You only have three legs," she said. "But I guess you know that."

There was something familiar about her, but I couldn't say just what. I followed her to the counter. The receptionist looked up.

"May I please talk to the vet?"

"Do you have an appointment?"

"No, it's about a lost dog, my lost dog, I don't mean lost, I mean I'm trying to find her and I heard about the shelter rescue and I just wanted to talk to her for a minute."

The girl's voice got wobbly at the end.

"One second," the receptionist said.

She stood up quickly and went to get MomDoc. The girl shifted from one foot to the other and back again, looking around at the people in the waiting room and picking at her fingernails. I wanted to do something to make her not so nervous, so I touched her leg with my nose and tilted my head that way that everyone says makes me look cute.

"Hi," she said, bending over to scratch behind my ears.

Did I ever tell you the best dog-people always know exactly where to scratch?

An old man with a birdcage in his lap nodded at me. "Ya know he's famous, right?"

"Because of his leg?"

"No, 'cuz of this!" He held a copy of the newspaper out and tapped the picture on the front. "See him right here? Unconfirmed rumor is he saved all them other dogs."

The girl took the paper and was studying the picture when MomDoc came out from the treatment area, but the girl didn't notice. Her eyes were pinned on the photograph, her mouth open. She gave a little gasp.

"Is that . . . that's Holly!"

MomDoc went to her and the girl looked up.

"That golden retriever in the front, is her name Holly?"

"Yes. She was a rescue from our shelter. Was she yours?" The girl nodded.

Betsy! It was Holly's Betsy! Oh, glorious day!

Oh, but Beth. What about Beth, who loved Holly, too?

"Come with me," MomDoc said. "Let's go to the office."

I followed on Betsy's heels. MomDoc closed the door almost

all the way to give her privacy because by this time she was full-out crying. MomDoc handed her the box of tissues from her desk.

"We moved and my parents left her behind, they told me we were coming back for her but they lied."

Betsy didn't abandon her. She loved her.

"I've cried about Holly every single day since we left. Is she okay?"

"She is, she is very much okay. She has a new home with a girl named Beth, they live next door to me and she is well loved."

Betsy gripped the edges of the newspaper and let tears stream down her cheeks. Her chest heaved and her hands shook and the paper got wet, but with all that, she was smiling in a big, happy, relieved kind of way.

"I'm so glad," she said. "Do you think she knows I love her? Or do you think she thought it was me who left her behind?"

MomDoc put her hand gently on Betsy's arm. "When she first came to the shelter she ran off. She was looking for someone. They found her down at the lake."

Betsy put her hand to her mouth. "That was our special place."

"She was looking for you, which tells me she knew it wasn't your fault. Be happy for her and know she is safe and loved and she will never get left behind again."

Betsy wiped her face with the back of her hand and smiled

up at MomDoc. "Thank you for telling me that. I needed to know. Do you think the new girl would let me see her? Even just once?"

"I can ask her. Give me your number and I'll pass it on. I think she'd be happy to know more about someone who loved Holly."

Betsy left with the newspaper gripped tight in her hands, and when she rode away, the pink ribbons streamed out from the handlebars of her bike.

"Well dang," the old man with the birdcage said. "She left with my paper."

MomDoc got another copy and handed it to him. "We've got plenty."

She looked out the clinic door as Betsy rode away, then stepped outside and picked up something from the ground. It was a tiny strip of pink plastic ribbon that had fallen from the bike. She tucked it into her pocket and smiled down at me by her feet.

"You did it, Di. You saved the world, just like I always knew you would."

My belly did that little tickle-flip thing again.

I love it when she says that.

AN AFTERWORD FROM DR. HEATHER CARLETON, THE REAL-LIFE MOMDOC

I have been a veterinarian for over twenty years and have seen thousands of animals in shelters over that time. Sadly, many of those animals have died because of lack of homes. On the flip side, I have seen thousands of purebred puppies that have been the fortunate ones—puppies who have been purchased to be the new family companion. I have always thought that shelters would empty if we would only stop intentionally breeding dogs for even just a few years.

All my pets have been rescues, and the real MahDi, Ozzie, Domino, and Koda are no different. MahDi and I first met at the Soi Dog Foundation, a shelter in Thailand that had over 250 dogs at the time. The same shelter today has over 1,500 dogs as a result of the continual influx of cruelty cases and abandoned pets.

As is described in the book, I knew MahDi and he knew me the minute we saw each other. He has been my three-legged companion for the last fourteen years—we can exchange looks and know exactly what the other is thinking. A bond with a dog is magical in that way.

I brought MahDi back to the United States with me during a difficult time in my life, and in his. He had been hit by a car in Thailand and lost his leg. When the veterinarian who had performed the operation told MahDi's owners he could go home, his owners said they did not want him anymore because he was no longer beautiful. The veterinarian then called John Dalley, who runs Soi Dog, and asked if he would take him. John agreed and brought MahDi to the shelter, convinced that he would become a "lifer" because of his amputation.

MahDi is the most beautiful dog, inside and out, I have ever seen. He has been there for me every day and there are not enough dog cookies in the world to let him know what he means to me.

It is my hope that this book will help raise awareness of all the good dogs, really good dogs, that either spend their lives waiting for a home or are put to sleep due to lack of space at the shelter. Although this is a work of fiction, many of the backstories of the dogs are based on the reality I have seen over the years as a veterinarian. *Heartbreaking* is only one adjective that comes to mind.

I raise my glass to all the amazing shelter workers who labor tirelessly to save and rehome abandoned dogs and cats. It is an emotionally exhausting responsibility, especially in shelters that have high euthanasia rates, because there are just too many animals to save them all. No one at a shelter ever wants to see an animal die. The only way to solve the problem of unwanted dogs and cats is through spaying and neutering and curbing the breeding of dogs. It is a simple solution. I hope the next generation accomplishes it.

MahDi means "good dog" in Thai—the literal translation is "dog good." MahDi, and all my rescues, have filled my life with humor, love, sacrifice, patience, and joy. I hope I can repay the favor.

—Dr. Heather Carleton

MahDi (left) and Ozzie (right)

ACKNOWLEDGMENTS

Near the end of 2020, that already tricky year of Covid, when I learned I was losing both my agent and my editor, I panicked. Over the years, I had developed trusting relationships with both my agent, Al Zuckerman, who rightfully retired at age ninety, and my brilliant editor, Andrew Eliopulos, who retired from publishing just a few months later. I didn't know what the change might mean to this book and all the wonderful animals whose voices deserve to be heard. But then I remembered what Mother Abbott always said: *When God closes a door, She always opens a window.*

Sure enough, in flew two equally brilliant visionaries, who encouraged me in just the right ways to keep working until we had this story just right. I am so humbled by the insight of my new agent, Susan Cohen at Writers House, who quickly proved to be not only wise and kind but also a cheerleader extraordinaire. And to my editor, Courtney Stevenson—I don't know if I can ever thank you enough for pushing me, for asking the questions, for keeping track of things I'd lost sight of along the way, and for seeing to it that this book was everything all the shelter animals in the world need it to be (and for always tucking in bits of humor that still have me giggling). To Rosemary Brosnan, who *gets* me, and whose wisdom matches me with the best of the best, you are amazing not only as an editor and mentor but as an extraordinary human being. You change lives. Many thanks to Christina Hess for bringing MahDi, Ozzie, and Domino to life on the cover of this book, and all the other people behind the scenes at both Writers House and HarperCollins/Quill Tree Books who make such good stuff happen, and whose support and encouragement and promotion help me sustain my literary life.

I am forever indebted to my friend Heather Carleton, DVM, for sharing this story with me, a story she knew needed to be out in the world. Over the years, I have watched her match dogs and cats with humans who needed them in the most remarkable ways. I have so many more stories to tell of people and animals whose lives were changed because of Heather's tireless work. Also, to Jerry Schendel, who quietly gave me encouragement at the moments I needed it, and who has the squishiest of dog-loving hearts. Thank you both.

This book wouldn't be what it is without my young beta-readers, Joy Hayashida-Ludington and Finna Halsey. Thank you for being enthusiastic voices and exceptionally tough critics. I am always inspired by my young friends at St. John's Episcopal Church Parent-Child Book Club, who teach me more than they know. I am humbled to be able to read with you every month.

To Lona Williams, who helped me breathe life into this story at a critical moment; to Clare Payne Symmons and Nicole Madison Garrett, who listened to me go on and on about this writing journey and who gave me encouragement and focus and never, ever let me doubt my ability to do justice to MahDi's story. Thank you to Jackson Hole Writers Conference and the young *Almost Authors* in our youth programs who motivate me to write the best stories I can. And to my sister-writers scattered near and far who shine like polished brass, hats off to you all.

My mom, Elizabeth, passed away while I was still writing this book, but I have faith she is somewhere in the universe holding hands with my dad and beaming. I know you are both proud of me and that means everything. To my beautiful sons, Parker and James. It is because you exist that I had the courage to learn to write. Special thanks to April North of Second Chance Rescue Ranch and Carrie Boynton of the

Animal Adoption Center, and all the thousands of rescue and shelter workers who put their heart and soul into saving animals every single day. Keep up the good fight. This book is written in memory of my very dear friend Liane Langbehn West (aka Leroi), who took in every homeless dog and human who crossed her path throughout her short life. Thank you for teaching me how to love that way.

And finally, to the real MahDi, Ozzie, and Koda, who, along with Domino and Sufi, sat beside me while I pounded away at my keyboard telling their stories and nudged me when I got weary. You saved some lives again today.